BROKEN ANCHOR

SINFUL TRUTHS BOOK 6

ELLA MILES

FREE BOOKS

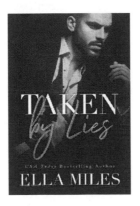

Read **Taken by Lies** for **FREE!** And sign up to get my latest releases, updates, and more goodies here→EllaMiles.com/freebooks

Follow me on **BookBub** to get notified of my new releases and recommendations here→Follow on BookBub Here

Join **Ella's Bellas FB group** to get **Pretend I'm Yours** for **FREE**→Join Ella's Bellas Here

TRUTH OR LIES WORLD

TRUTH OR LIES SERIES:

SINFUL TRUTHS SERIES:

PROLOGUE

ZEKE

HOW FAR WILL I go for love?

That's the question that stays with me as I float, bobbing up and down over waves that could easily consume me. I've been here before; been in this same dire situation. Felt like I can't breathe, like this is the end.

My blood is slipping from my body. My ribs are tightening around my lungs like a vise grip. My head is raging in a bone-spitting headache from all the pain I feel.

The only pain I care about, though, emanates from my heart.

Last time I was here, in the darkness of night, in the middle of the vast ocean, I was content. I was dying to save Kai and Enzo, my family, those I love.

This time, I'm dying to save my one true love.

I thought I knew what dying for someone felt like. But this—this is so much more. This is different. This is what I was put on this earth to do—to die protecting someone I love.

I've always been a protector.

That is who I am.

I could change careers, but it wouldn't change who I am. I, Zeke Kane, am a protector. I am only me when I'm protecting others.

I've protected many people in my life—sacrificed over and over again. But I've never risked it all like I did to protect Siren.

I've never hurt someone I love in order to protect Siren.

Never sinned like I did to protect Siren.

I would do it all again.

I would end up right here back in this ocean if it meant I got to love Siren like I did. That I got the honor of protecting her, saving her, even though she didn't need me to save her. She never did; she was always enough for herself.

She tried to tell me all along—trust her, let her save herself. That way, I wouldn't have to give up myself.

Siren didn't understand that I wanted to give up everything for her. The only way I could love her was to love her with everything, even knowing that our love would destroy everything.

For a moment, Siren thought I turned my back on our love. She thought I was ashamed of what I did. It took her all of five minutes to figure out my lie.

I would never turn my back on our love. And I would do all the horrible sins over again, if it were the only way to keep her and our unborn child safe.

My only regret is that I can't love her forever. That I have to give her up. That one day she will find another man to make her happy. And when I haunt her ass from hell, I won't even be upset that she found happiness. She's made so many sacrifices; she deserves all the happiness in the world.

It makes dying easier—knowing that Siren gets to live. I

will take her sins with me when I die. She will get to live in truth, in love, in happiness.

How far am I willing to go for love?

Too far.

How much am I willing to break?

All the way.

We've all sinned.

Enzo.

Kai.

Langston.

Liesel.

Siren.

Me.

All of us.

We've all hurt each other in unforgivable ways while protecting those we hold dearest. And that's the way it should be. None of us hold grudges for what Enzo did to protect Kai. What Langston did for Liesel. Or what I did for Siren.

In the end, we protect our own.

We all do what has to be done to protect the love of our lives.

We are all a family. And we fix our mistakes.

I'm leaving this earth knowing my family forgives me for the sins I've caused.

And I forgive them. All of them.

In a game of truth or sin, we all chose sin.

The truth broke us.

Love destroyed us.

Sin saved us.

How far will I go for love?

As far as it takes...

1

ZEKE

S<small>IREN IS SAFE</small>.

My child is safe.

They are safe.

That's what I repeat over and over again as I step into the helicopter following Julian. That's the only thing keeping my feet moving.

I walked away from Siren. We hardly spoke before I left her, but we both knew what it meant. That I wasn't coming back—either because I'll die protecting my family or do something so horrible that Siren won't want me back.

It's a lie.

It's all a lie.

I can pretend all I want that I'll die in battle with Julian, or that the best thing for Siren is to live without me. I tell myself I can stand to leave her to find a new man—one who hasn't murdered for her.

Lies.

Siren is my everything. The reason I'm still alive. The reason I'm getting into this damn helicopter.

And as for the sins I've committed, I would commit

them all again. I would shoot Enzo again. I would betray my friends again. I would betray every person on this planet in order to protect Siren and my child.

If that makes me a monster, so be it. I'm a monster. I'm a horrible friend. I've betrayed everyone who was ever good to me.

I look at the man standing in front of me—a man smirking like he's won. Julian Reed is the devil. But when I put a bullet into Enzo, not knowing if he was going to survive or not, I became the devil too. It doesn't matter that I was doing it to save us. It doesn't matter that I shot him to protect Siren. It doesn't matter that I did everything in my power to ensure that Enzo lives.

I shot one of my best friends.

Then I shoved him over the edge of the yacht and left him to die.

My stomach tightens, threatening to spill at the thought.

No, Enzo Black is alive. I did everything I could to protect my friend. He's alive. Kai will find him. She'll realize what we did.

I won't have to ask for Enzo or Kai's forgiveness this time, but what if there's a next time? How far will I go for Siren?

As far as it takes to keep her safe.

Which is why I'm here, on Julian's helicopter, committing my loyalty to him. It's why I left Siren alone—to fulfill my destiny to protect her and our baby at all costs.

So I'm going to do this. I'm going to help Julian. Then, I'm going to kill Julian, Bishop, and any other man who threatens to hurt Siren or my baby. Finally, I'm going to spend the rest of my life loving Siren like it's my job, my reason for existence. And I don't care how many people we burn with our love.

I strap myself into the seat next to Julian in the second

row. The propellers spin overhead, buzzing loudly in my ear. I pick up headphones and cover my ear, muting the sound.

We lift off, and my heart cracks, leaving Siren behind.

She's safe.

Our baby is safe.

That's why I'm doing this—to keep her safe.

Langston will protect her as well as I could. He'll get her the fuck away from all the danger.

Kai and Enzo will come. They will fight. They are too invested not to.

But Siren will be safe with Langston. He promised me he would keep her safe. He has no one else to live for, so he'll live for her. Protect her like he loves her.

I thought Langston was in love with Liesel. I thought he would be the next to get his happily ever after. I guess I was wrong.

But I trust that Langston will keep his word.

I glance down, my first mistake. Siren is on the top deck of the yacht, staring up at me with so much pain and sadness in her eyes.

I had to, baby. I had to give up myself to keep you safe. I had to turn into a monster, the devil. You can be a little devilish too. And when I return, our darkness will blend together. We will heal each other.

She grips her biceps as if holding herself back from running after me. It's not like she has another option; she can't chase after a helicopter on foot. Although, I wouldn't put it past her to dive into the ocean and swim stride for stride keeping up with the helicopter. That's how incredible she is.

I look at her sternly out the window. *This sacrifice will all be for nothing if you follow me. Stay safe. Protect our baby.*

Her eyes tell me I'm wrong. Her eyes tell me I've made a mistake.

She screams, I think, or maybe she sings. I can't tell from the whirl of the helicopter blades. But I can feel her pain hit my heart.

I know, baby. I know. This will all be over soon, though. Just wait a little longer.

I watch as Langston walks up behind her.

She's safe. I glare at him with my most dangerous threat. *If you survive and she doesn't, the first thing I'm going to do is kill you.*

Langston smirks, but there is a heaviness behind his eyes.

What am I missing?

Nothing. I'm just being paranoid—Siren is safe with Langston.

Julian leans his head to look out the window, and then he looks back at me. He does this over and over again. And then he's chuckling, wildly, madly. His wretched chuckle rings in my ear thanks to the headphones we are using to communicate with each other.

"What's so funny?" I ask, assuming he's not going to tell me.

"Who is that man standing behind Aria?" Julian asks.

I frown. "Langston."

"Bishop," Julian says simultaneously.

It all clicks.

Everything I've been too stupid to see. The reason that Langston has been gone this whole time. It's not because he was chasing after a girl. It's because he was busy working with Julian. He was busy turning on his friends, betraying us all in a way that makes me shooting Enzo look like exchanging friendship bracelets instead of the stark betrayal it was.

Langston is working with our enemy. What he did to Siren's head. What he could have done to her body. Tricking me into thinking he will protect her instead of using her in some grand scheme with Julian Reed.

"You bastard," I curse as I try to figure out my next move. Apparently, my next move is choking the man next to me; consequences be dammed. I can't actually kill Julian, though. This was his security plan all along—have Langston, or Bishop, whoever he is, watch Siren and hurt or kill her if I don't do as Julian says.

So I can't kill Julian, but I can hurt him a little.

Julian shakes his head, and that's when I realize the man sitting next to the pilot has a gun on my head.

I release him.

"You promised Siren would be safe," I bark as I unhook my seatbelt even though a gun is still pointed at my head.

I have to get to Siren. She's not safe. Not with that lying asshole. He hurt her already. He fucked with her head. I never thought I would want to kill a man who I grew up with. A man that a few moments ago, I would have done anything to protect. Langston is like a brother to me. But Langston is dead. Bishop took over.

Why? What happened to turn him into this cruel man?

I don't know.

And I don't care. I just want to put a bullet in his head for hurting Siren. Just like I want to burn Julian at the stake for raping her.

Before I think it through, I have the door of the helicopter open, and I'm staring down at the ocean below. We've flown far enough away from Siren and Langston that I can barely make them out in the distance. We are flying too high above the ocean. If I jump, there is no guarantee that I'll survive.

Fuck.

I grab the gun out of the asshole's hand in the front seat and have it aimed at Julian so fucking fast.

Julian just grins. We've been here so many times. And he knows just like all the others, I won't pull the trigger. If he dies, there is nothing stopping Bishop from killing Siren a second later.

"Turn this helicopter around," I say.

"You really think I planned this?"

"Yes. You two have been working together this whole time. Turn this the fuck around. I didn't agree to work for you while you let your guard dog watch Siren and kill her if I put one toe out of line."

Julian considers his next words carefully, which puts me on edge. *Is he concocting a lie? Or trying to figure out some way to prevent me from killing him?*

"Turn this helicopter around now. Or I'll kill you and your men, then turn the helicopter around myself. This wasn't part of our arrangement. I work for you; Siren is safe. This is the opposite of Siren being safe."

"Bishop doesn't work for me."

"Bullshit."

Julian laughs. "Really? Bishop, or Langston, whatever his name is, was loyal to you a lot longer than he's ever been loyal to me. What makes you think his loyalty lies with me and not you?"

"The fact that he hurt Siren."

A sly grin works its way over Julian's features. His words only had one goal—get me to remember just how dangerous Bishop is; realize just how much danger Siren is in.

"Shoot me and find out whose side Bishop is on."

I hold the gun right up to his forehead. He doesn't try to bat my hand away. He knows that even though Bishop is definitely on Julian's side now, I can't shoot Julian. It's too risky. I can't kill Julian, kill the two men in the front of this helicopter, and return to Siren before Bishop kills her.

Bishop staying with Siren is their insurance policy that I behave. That I do what they want. That I hurt everyone I love for them.

"Tell Bishop to let Siren go."

Julian cracks his neck. So cavalier with his own life. So sure that I won't kill him. I won't kill him today, but it doesn't mean I won't kill him soon. His day is coming. And then I'll commit the ultimate sin, and I'll enjoy every second of it.

"Tell him," I command, my threat clear in my voice.

"No."

I fire, purposefully grazing the top of his head, so the bullet only burns over his hair, searing it and leaving a permanent mark on the top of his head, but not seriously wounding him.

But it does what I intended—send fear into him. Fear that I will actually kill him.

I kill the man in the passenger seat, and then I shoot the pilot before I jump out of the helicopter, grabbing the landing gear under the helicopter and hanging from it.

I know that if Siren can see me, I'm probably causing her a heart attack right now. So I hope that she can't. For once, I hope that Bishop has her tied her up in a bedroom or the yacht has turned and driven far enough away that she can't see me.

I don't have time to think about Siren right now. I'm dangling from the bottom of a helicopter that is going down, at least until Julian gets into the pilot's seat and takes control.

I have to time this just right. I have to wait until the helicopter has descended far enough down that it is safe for me to jump, but not wait too long so that Julian has gained control again and started ascending.

I stare at the dark ocean beneath me getting closer with each second. I know we need to be at least 200 feet in order for me to jump safely and have a good chance at survival.

Just a little lower.

Come on.

I glance up, but all I can see is the bottom of the helicopter. I have no idea what is happening inside. I don't know how close Julian is to getting control of the helicopter.

So close. Just...

The helicopter starts yanking up. This is my chance.

I'll do anything to keep Siren safe. Including risking my own life.

I let go.

Falling, having no idea if I'm close enough to the water to safely jump, but I risk it.

I don't have a choice.

If I don't jump, if I don't do everything I can to protect Siren, I might as well die. Siren is my only reason for living.

The three-second fall seems to last a lot longer. In that time, I think about everything.

Every sin Siren and I have committed against each other.

Every sin we've committed for each other.

I think about our unborn child.

Cayden.

He has Siren's eyes. And my chin.

He has the name of a hero. A name that gives him the power to fight.

Siren and I haven't talked names, and I don't even know if the child she carries is a boy or a girl. But the name is clear in my mind when I hit the water.

It's clear when I sink twenty feet under the water.

It's clear when I kick my legs, propelling my body up.

It's clear when I take a deep breath after I crack the surface.

Cayden.

The name means fighter.

He's my fighter.

If fighting to protect Siren wasn't enough, now I have a second reason. I may not be strong enough to protect everyone—Siren, my son, and my extended family. But my son is. Siren is.

I'll do everything I can to protect them—everything.

2

SIREN

I STAND ON THE DECK, watching the helicopter fly away with Zeke and the devil. I'm left with a man who might be worse than the devil.

"Come on," Bishop says.

I laugh at his craziness. "Just like that, huh? You think you can control me because you've fucked with my head. Given me endless nightmares. You're going to have to do better than that."

"No, I won't."

"Yes, you will. You'll have to drug me. Tie me up. Because unless you are taking me to go after my husband, I'm not coming with you."

"Your husband, huh?"

I frown, folding my arms over my chest as I glare at Bishop, flashing him my wedding ring.

Bishop doesn't react. "So sure of your love. So sure of his." It's not a question. He says it because he knows it's how I feel. He's mocking me, acting like I shouldn't be sure about anything, definitely not my love for Zeke and his love for me.

14

We stare at each other in an unspoken standoff.

"Have I ever hurt you, Siren?"

"Yes."

"You sure about that?" His brows raise, and a wicked grin flicks across his lips.

What is he getting at? Have I imagined everything he's done to me?

I try to think, but as soon as I do, my head clouds. The more I think about what Bishop did, the foggier it gets.

"You hurt me. You tortured me. You fucked with my head."

Bishop nods. "If you are sure..."

He's playing games. Don't fall for it. He's fucking with my head. I need to do the same back.

"How could you do it? How could you betray your best friend?"

He gets in my face. A gentle rage flows from his body as he crowds me, but doesn't touch me. "How could you betray the man you love?"

I suck in a breath.

My world spins on its axis. *Have I judged Bishop wrongly this whole time? Has he just been doing what he had to do to survive? To keep us safe? To make Julian think he was on his side? Or is he manipulating me now to get what he wants? To get me to go with him without a fight?*

"Who are you?"

"You already know." Tension leaves him as he speaks.

"Are you Bishop or Langston?"

His lips thin, and he turns, walking away from me as he heads inside the yacht.

I follow.

He goes into the bridge, starts the engines, and starts driving us away. I don't try to stop him.

"Are you good or evil?"

He chuckles. "Really? What are we, five? You of all people know there is no such thing as a person being all good or all evil."

I do, but I also know that every person still thinks of themselves as all good or all evil. Good people sometimes do bad things, and evil people sometimes do good. But in our deepest hearts, we all see ourselves as one or the other.

How does Bishop see himself?

He isn't going to tell me, at least not right now.

"Where are we going?"

"Where do you think?"

I shrug. "I honestly don't know. I don't know who you are or what to think of you."

"We are going to get the box with the vials of cancer virus and cure in it."

I frown.

"No."

"You're not the one in charge. You won't be making the decisions. All the decisions you made were wrong anyway."

"What's that supposed to mean?"

"You working for Julian and hurting Zeke—it doesn't seem like the kind of thing a person does if they love someone."

My blood boils. I charge at him.

"How dare you!" I hit him. I meant to just slap him, but it becomes a punch. I don't think about all the reasons I shouldn't be punching him. I just punch. I fight. *How dare he question my love for Zeke!* He has no idea how hard it was. No idea what I've done to save Zeke.

"I love Zeke with everything! Everything I've done has been to protect him! Don't you understand that? The only two men I've ever made a vow to were my ex-husband and

Zeke. I promised Julian everything to keep Zeke alive. Julian can't kill Zeke!"

Bishop grabs my wrists, stopping me from throwing another punch. It dawns on me that he never punched me back. He never stopped me. He took every punch. He let me hurt him.

Why?

Who is Langston Bishop? I doubt Bishop is Langston's last name. Zeke and Kai and Enzo would have gotten suspicious at the first mention of Bishop's name if so. But in my head, this man standing in front of me is both Langston and Bishop. Both good and bad. More bad than good, but there is a part of him that was once good. A part that was once loyal to Enzo Black. To Kai Black. To Zeke Kane.

I just have to find that man again.

Who are you? I think as I stare up at the man still gripping my wrists with force, but not hard enough to hurt me, just enough to prevent me from hitting him again.

"A man you are going to have to trust if you want to survive this," he answers.

I thought I asked the question in my head, but apparently not. That, or he can now read my thoughts.

I jerk my wrists out of his. "There is no way I'll ever trust a man who has hurt me."

Langston Bishop looks at me with a stern gaze. Somehow he seems taller, his shoulders broader, his intensity deeper. Zeke is a giant among men. Langston's blonde hair, fair skin, and slimmer build make me think he was once the light. The casual man. The playboy, if I understood correctly from everyone's stories about him.

Right now, Langston Bishop is the opposite of light. He's darkness.

But so are you, Siren...

He shrugs his shoulders and rolls his eyes at me, pretending to not care whether or not I trust him, but it's a front. The darkness, the pain is covering something deeper. It could be darker, more evil than the shield he's wearing like armor, or it could be the light that he long ago buried.

He shakes his head. "This is all your fault, you know?"

I frown. "My fault. Really? I was blackmailed by Julian. Basically sold to him by my ex-husband. I was tortured by you. Raped by Julian. Trust me, none of this is my fault."

He snickers as if he has a secret so obvious he can't believe I haven't realized it yet.

"What?" I ask, needing to understand, needing the truth.

"It doesn't matter that you didn't want any of it. Neither did Helen of Troy, and yet a war was fought for her."

"I'm not Helen of Troy."

"No, you're a siren—much more dangerous. You are capable of destroying us all if you wanted to."

I frown. I agree. I could hurt them all. Kill them all. I know how powerful I can be when I'm angry. I know the depths I will go if I'm pushed. If I had wanted to kill them all, then they would already be dead.

I was the only one who could have killed Julian Reed in the beginning. Instead, I found a different way to save Zeke, and in the end, it could cost us all our lives.

"Which is why I'm glad you're on my team," Langston Bishop says, turning back toward the helm, and we start moving again.

"I'm not on your team."

"Yes, you are. We all want the same thing—the box. Whoever has it wins the war. I know you wouldn't have chosen me as your partner. Trust me, you are the last person I would have chosen as well, but this is where the cards lay. We all go after the box. Julian and Zeke, Kai and Enzo, you and me. Once we win, then we can figure out which of us gets to use it."

"I'm not on your side. And I'm not going to help you steal the box. It belongs to Kai and Enzo."

"You'll help because you love him. There is no way you won't help."

Langston Bishop doesn't believe me. He's going to drag me into the middle of a fight I have no business being in. I can't fight when I have another life to worry about.

"You're wrong."

"I'm not."

"I'm pregnant."

Langston cuts the engine at my words and slowly turns to face me with shock on his face. His brain is working into overdrive, trying to figure out what to do with this information—with me.

"Who knows?" he asks, staring down at my stomach, and trying to figure out how he missed the swell of my stomach before.

"Everyone."

His teeth grind together. I don't know why it matters who knows. Everyone knowing is a good thing. It means that only the cruelest would attack a pregnant woman, and I'm not even sure Julian is that evil.

"Julian?" he asks.

I shrug. "I doubt it unless Zeke told him."

Langston Bishop's eyes move side to side as he thinks. "Good, make sure to keep it that way."

"Why? Why does it matter if Julian knows?"

"Because he'll either try to claim it as his own or kill it." His words are solemn like it hurts him to say them, which confuses me even more. He turns back and starts moving us away again.

He doesn't order me around.

He doesn't tell me what to do.

He said we were teammates.

I'm more confused than ever.

I need to remember everything that Langston Bishop has done to me. I need to remember how he fucked with my head. I need him to fix me. I need to run and hide until the danger is over.

I brush my hand over my stomach, where my baby resides. It still doesn't feel real.

I will protect my baby with my life. But Langston Bishop is right; there is no way I'm going to stay out of this fight. Not when Zeke's life is on the line.

3

KAI

I HIT the water minutes after Zeke shoots Enzo. I already know the outcome before I jump into the water. I know—I feel Enzo's vibration the second my body hits the water. I may have a strange, unreal connection with Zeke, but my connection with Enzo is otherworldly.

Enzo Black is my husband, my best friend, the father of my children. He's the strongest man I know—a man who is strong despite having an equally strong wife who technically holds more power than him.

We've always been able to take down our enemies together. As long as we are together, we are strong. Unstoppable. Together we win. But apart, that's when we lose. Being together isn't about being physically together. Being together is about sharing our hearts. Enzo and I share one heart, one set of lungs, one of everything. We are one person in two bodies.

Despite the pain and turmoil it seems we have caused each other, this is far from the worst day of our lives. This doesn't even scratch the surface.

Our greatest enemies are our friends. Those who love

us, also have that one special person that they love more. That they have to protect above everything else. That's when our lives are at risk.

Which is why we're prepared—for everything. Even the greatest betrayal.

It doesn't ease the anxiety ripping through my chest and taking over my mind. Even though I know the outcome, my anxiety doesn't, and it's the part of me in control. It's driving me forward, propelling me to swim faster when there is no need.

Finally, the sight I needed to see to crush my anxiety for good comes into view—Enzo.

He's in the water, floating on his back, looking up at the dark sky.

I take a deep breath and swim toward him. I may have had a temporary moment of anxiety and fear, but I won't let Enzo see that.

"You're a good actor," I say, keeping my voice light and playful when I approach him.

Enzo continues to float on his back for a second longer. My words didn't startle him. He felt me coming before I spoke. Before the waves my swimming created washed over him, he knew I was coming.

"And you're a terrible actor," he says, smirking as he comes to face me.

I pout, hating being terrible at anything. "I am not! Julian thought I was concerned about you dying."

I try to keep my hands to myself as I tread water instead of checking him out all over like I want to, but the fact that he's joking with me tells me he's more than fine—our plan worked.

Enzo smiles at me as his hand brushes my hair from my face, finally giving me the touches I'm desperately craving.

"I'm not talking about then. I'm talking about now," he says.

I shudder. "I'm not acting."

"Yes, you are. You're pretending you are strong. That you were one hundred percent certain that our plan worked and you just calmly swam over here. When in truth, the second you started acting in front of Julian, your anxiety hit a new level, and you couldn't squash it. Even though you knew deep down that I would be fine, your anxiety took over, and you're afraid and pissed and need me."

I scowl at him. But of course, he's right.

"Yes, I fucking need you! You're my husband, my everything. And I had a full-on panic attack swimming to you that I would find your corpse instead of finding you relaxedly floating on your back. I—"

Enzo's lips crash down on mine. They are desperate, hungry, and tells me I wasn't the only one acting. I know him letting Zeke push him over the edge of the yacht was hard, because it meant he left me unprotected.

Apart we are vulnerable—together, we are unstoppable.

His tongue pushes into my mouth, and my hands grip his face before sliding down his neck. I need to make sure that he's okay.

"You're okay? You're not hurt?" I ask, before diving in for another kiss. If he isn't okay, if he's really hurt, I shouldn't be kissing him like this. I shouldn't be stealing all his breaths. But I can't help myself. I need his kisses. I need to know that we are more than okay.

"Yes. Are you okay?" he asks, his voice deepening into a protective beast that will swim the length of the ocean to kill Julian if I'm hurt.

I grin against his lips. "I just swam a good hundred yards. I'm kissing my husband. I'm good."

"Thank fuck."

And then we are kissing and kissing and kissing.

We are still treading water, while our hands confirm what our words said—that we are okay.

I start first, yanking off his shirt that is covered in what I hope is fake blood. Enzo's hands slink under my shirt, rips apart my bulletproof vest, and then feels the skin over my stomach before cupping my breasts.

I gasp as he does. "I'm fine."

He smirks. "I know. But I think I need to fuck you to be sure."

My body heats. *God, I need to fuck him.* I need to feel connected to him completely. I need to know that the connection we share is still as strong as ever.

"Yes," the word is a plea, a promise, a cry. I need Enzo inside me. I need to feel connected. I need us to be us again.

No more pretending.

No more acting.

No more lying, scheming, betraying. That's not who we are. We tell each other the truth. We share everything. And that's not going to stop now. No matter how we hurt each other.

I kiss him again hard, but we can't fuck here in the middle of the ocean while treading water. So as much as I want to keep kissing and kissing, we need to stop and come up with a plan to find land or a boat, something.

But before we go anywhere, I need to know...

Enzo growls, seeing the concern etched on my face. I know I got a dozen more gray hairs and a couple more worry lines in the last hour alone.

"Look, I'm fine. The bullet hit the armor and exploded the fake blood bag just like we planned."

He's fine.

The bullet didn't hit him.
The blood is fake.
He was just acting when he wheezed.
He's just bruised from the impact of the bullet.
Zeke didn't shoot him.
Zeke is his friend.
He knew.
He knew about the bulletproof vests and jackets.
He was wearing one himself.
Enzo was never in any danger.
He's fine.

"Stingray, look…"

Enzo grabs my hands and runs it over his jacket. He shows me where the bullets are lodged in the armor. He shows me the fake blood oozing from it. Then he removes the jacket and puts my hand on the spots where the bullets should have entered his body but didn't.

I find no holes.

Enzo is fine. He's alive. The bullet didn't even break his skin.

And then the tears fall.

The anxiety, fear, panic all take their toll, and finally, I burst in one big release. I clutch onto Enzo's neck as the tears cascade down my face, and my cries fall from my lips in waves that I'm sure can be heard for miles around.

Enzo holds me tight to his chest as he kisses my cheeks, catching each tear before it falls to the ocean.

"It's okay, I got you," Enzo says.

I can barely process his words, but somehow we are moving. We are swimming. And then I'm being pulled up onto a boat. One of our yachts, I realize.

"Where to?" Ethan, one of our men, asks me.

"Miami," Enzo answers.

"Do you need medical assistance first?"

"No, we'll be in the captain's room," Enzo answers before lifting me against his bare wet chest and carrying me through the yacht to the captain's room at the back.

"We shouldn't kick Griffin out of his room," I say as Enzo enters in a code and the door opens.

"It's the most secure room on the ship. We are kicking him out of the room," he growls.

When the door shuts, we collapse on the bed. Enzo's lips collide with mine again, and I forget about kicking Griffin out of the room. I forget about the new danger we face. I forget about our friends that we should be worried about protecting. All I can think about is Enzo and our kids.

"Ellie, Finn?" I ask, trying to be a good mother, but Enzo is making it hard as he kisses down my neck.

"They are safe. Nora and Beckett have them. They would call if there was a problem."

They are safe.

My shirt is off, and then he pauses over me.

I shiver underneath him, not because we are both soaked, but because of Enzo's stare. Even after all this time together, after everything we've been through, one look from Enzo still makes me feel like an inexperienced virgin about to be taken for the first time. One touch from him sends my toes curling, my heart racing. One kiss and I become consumed by him.

And Enzo knows it.

But just because he makes me feel alive and protected in a way that I've never felt before, I'm still pissed at him.

"You let Siren kiss you."

My fingers rake down his front, my nails teasing his skin before I get to his soaked jeans.

He sucks in a breath when I roughly undo the button on his jeans, followed by the zipper.

"Stingray," he says my name like a warning. I know how this works. We both like it rough. And we have no problem taking what we need from each other—punishing each other when it's deserved—loving each other sweetly when the mood is right. And right now, this won't be about making love. This will be a fierce, intense grind of punishment, sin, and love. Once I start, once I declare that punishment needs to be given, I'll unleash his monster inside him —it's exactly what I want.

"You. Kissed. Her."

I reach into his pants and grab his rock hard member.

"Kai," he growls, his voice so gruff and husky as he tries to keep control of the situation.

I'm not mad. Not really. I know that Enzo loves me. I know I'm the only woman for him. I know that he only let Siren kiss him so he could understand who Siren is, what her intentions are, how far she will go. But right now, when my emotions are this high, I want a reason to give him everything I have—my good and bad.

I squeeze too hard.

"Do you deny it?"

I bite my lip as I meet him eye to eye. I know what happened. I was there. I saw. But I want him to say it. I want to hear him speak his crime. Even if he committed the crime for the right reason, it still needs to be punished. Just like Zeke will one day pay for shooting Enzo. Even though it ultimately saved his life. Even though he did it to save Siren. All sins catch up to us eventually.

We all sin.

We all lie.

"No, I don't deny it."

I slide my hand up and down his cock, letting him know

that I have all the power. I'm in complete control here, not him, as I let my nails dance over the skin of his cock.

He hisses but doesn't stop me, even though he's bigger than me. He lets me hurt him. He sinned. He let Siren kiss him. He let her lips touch what was mine.

And now, I'm going to make him pay. I'm going to commit my own sin against my husband. And we are both going to enjoy every minute of it.

4

ENZO

KAI STROKES ME AGAIN. Her nails dig deeper into my flesh.

I've hurt Kai before.

I've done unimaginable things, betrayed her too many times, but never with her as my wife. When we took those vows, she became mine, and I became hers. We've never seriously threatened the vows we took, never tested the wedding bands we wear, never pushed the limits of what it means to be married.

But I did.

I let another woman kiss me. I hurt my wife. Now I'm going to let her get her revenge. I'm going to do everything I can to let her heal. She needs this. I need this.

I need my stingray back. I need to be worthy of her love again.

Suddenly, she stops. Her hand is no longer on my cock, and for a second, I think she's changed her mind. We aren't going to fuck. She isn't going to punish me for hurting her, even for a good reason.

"Stingray, please."

She bites her lip at my soft plea. Then she runs her hand through her dark hair as she lays on the bed.

"What are you doing?"

She's silent. It takes me two seconds to realize what she is doing. I may have fucked up, but I'm still her husband. I still know her better than anyone. I know what she's thinking, sometimes even before she does.

This silence, this unspeaking, this untouching—this is my punishment.

It's her punishment, too, though. She can pretend she can hold out as much as I can, or that she doesn't want to fuck me after I let another woman kiss me. She's wrong. She wants to fuck me. She wants to feel our connection again. She needs it as much as I do.

"You can punish me all you want, Stingray. Dig your nails into me. Deny me orgasms. Whip me. Beat me. Pour hot wax onto my body. Tie me up. Do your worst. But don't you dare deny what you deserve. Use my body. Take care of yourself. Take out your pain on me. But don't you dare feel a second of pain in the process."

One.

Two.

And then, a smile. This is what she was waiting for—me to surrender, me to give her my full permission to do her worst.

I grin back even though I know what my stingray is capable of. I don't know how upset she really is about the kiss. I only let the kiss happen to find out what Siren was up to. Kai knows that, but she needs to hear it from me. She needs to understand how much letting another woman kiss me hurt me, and how much it felt like nothing compared to kissing her.

Kai needs to know I will never want another woman; I only want her.

Forever.

Nothing will ever stop me from loving her.

I stand up and let my pants drop until I'm completely naked in front of her. My chest is bruised from where the bullets hit me, but the way Kai's eyes are eating up my body, I know I must not look too bad.

I smirk.

"You want me."

She frowns and then stands, removing her own pants until she's naked in front of me.

"I shouldn't." She gives me a stern look. Her eyes narrow, her lips tense, and her jaw hardens.

I put my hands out in front of her. "Tie me up. Hurt me. Make me pay for what I did to you."

Her fingers trace over my wrists lightly, imagining ties around them, I'm sure. It drives me mad. I feel her light touch warm my body. Her touch ripples over my skin and hardens my cock.

I don't know what we will find in Griffin's closet, but I'd guess we could at least find a tie. If we are lucky, some rope or handcuffs.

"No," she snaps, removing her hands from my skin.

"No?" I step closer into her space, practically begging her to touch me. She can't resist my rockhard body, just like I can't resist her soft curves.

She bats her eyelashes at me as heat fills her cheeks. "I don't need to tie you up. You're my husband. You'll do what I say. You'll take your punishment without moving."

She's right. I will. I'd rather be tied up though, it would be easier. It's going to drive me crazy to let her touch me and not touch her back.

"On the bed, hubby."

I swallow the knot in my throat. It's not fear, I feel, but regret. I should have found a different way to find out what Siren was up to. I shouldn't have fucked with our wedding vows. I shouldn't have tested Kai's love for me.

I walk to the bed and lay down face up.

"Turn over."

I give her a suspicious look but do as she says. I roll onto my stomach.

"You do realize that thing you need to make yourself feel good is on the other side of my body, right?"

She chuckles. "I understand geometry. I know that I can't ride your cock with you on your stomach. I'm not ready to fuck you yet."

Her words slice through me. I don't know what she has planned, but I saw a twinkle in her eye, and I know that look means trouble.

Outside I growl, but inside I'm smiling. This is the woman I married—a woman stronger than me. A woman who knows what she wants and expects of me and will settle for nothing less. I love this woman with everything I have.

I let my eyes wander around the room, trying to find something she could use to punish me. I see a lamp, a pen, a remote. Not really what I was hoping to find. No candle. No rope. And not shockingly, no whips.

Kai moves onto the bed and then straddles my hips before her hands come down on my shoulders like she's about to give me a massage. I tense because I know better, rather than relax.

"Why so tense? You have no reason to feel tense, baby. Just like I had no reason to be tense after seeing your lips pressed against another woman."

She massages for a second before her claws dig into my skin like daggers. My shoulder is sore from being shot there. Even though the bullet didn't impact my skin, the deep bruise hurts when she squeezes.

She leans down until her hot breath is on my neck, and I groan. It feels so good. For a second, I forget she wants to punish me as she kisses down my neck. When her kisses get to my back, she changes from kissing to sinking her teeth into me.

My groans turn painful as she bites me over and over, all over my back. I'm going to have dozens of bite marks all over my back.

"You. Are. Mine."

I smile, loving how possessive she is of me.

She moves down until she is at my ass, and when she bites down on my cheek, I can't help but yelp.

She smacks over where she just bit me. "Mine."

"Yours, baby. I'm all yours."

"You sure about that?"

"Yes."

"Every inch of you?"

"Yes."

"What about this part of you?" She licks her fingers before circling them over my asshole.

I clench, not wanting her to touch me there. She never has before. We are pretty wild in the bedroom. We've done almost everything, except that.

But if she needs to know that all of me is hers, I'm up for trying anything with her.

"Yes, all of me is yours."

And then her finger is pushing inside me, claiming all of me. At first, it feels incredibly uncomfortable. My eyes even water at the intrusion. She doesn't give me time to get used to the feeling until another finger is inside and then another.

She finds my prostate and strokes me until the pain turns to pleasure.

Holy fuck, it feels good.

My cock hardens, and I'm desperate for her.

I move, trying to grab her. To feel her. To make her feel good.

But she slaps my hand away.

"Don't move."

She continues to push into me until I'm so close to coming. And then suddenly she stops.

"Turn over."

I do, resisting all my natural urges to touch her.

"Your ass is mine, but what about your lips? Are they mine?"

"Yours. They are all yours."

"You sure about that? Because I'm pretty sure I saw you kissing another woman with these lips."

"Let me show you how much I didn't give her. I didn't give her what matters."

I grab her hips without permission and pull her until she is straddling my face, and then I drive my tongue between her legs until I taste her sweetness. She rides my face as I lick her lips slowly with my tongue, spreading her wider.

"Jesus," she purrs as I find her clit and flick it with careful precision.

She's lost control as I remind her how much she owns my lips and tongue, show her what I haven't given to any woman but her.

Her back arches, and she grabs the headboard behind me as I devour her. She reacts so quickly to my actions. I can feel all of her wetness cover my lips and tongue just like I wanted. Her lips swell, along with her clit, and her sweetness spills onto my tongue.

But it's not enough. I want to make her scream. I reach up and grab her breasts, flicking over her nipples in a circular way that I know drives her mad.

"Enzo!" And then I claim her. I remind her that she alone owns my lips as she comes all over my face.

Slowly, she comes down from her high. She remembers that she is supposed to be punishing me, not letting me enjoy myself. She carefully climbs off my face and moves back until she is just above my cock.

Yes, please fuck me. Feeling her come over my face is one of my favorite things—watching her come undone like that.

But there is nothing like being inside her. I don't need to come. I don't care about my pleasure. I just need to feel the connection between us.

"What about this?" She grabs my cock. "Is this still mine and mine alone?"

Her voice has changed. Gone is the lightheartedness. Gone is the teasing. She's pissed.

I frown, hating that I made her feel this way for even a single second.

"My cock is always only yours. I've never strayed, and I never will."

She grabs it again, holding it rougher than usual as she pumps me hard.

"She touched you."

"She didn't."

"I saw. Her hand was in your pants."

"She didn't touch me. Her finger grazed me on accident, but that was it. She. Didn't. Touch. Me. I wouldn't have let her. That would have been too far. It would have crossed a

35

line that even I wouldn't have been able to forgive myself for."

She hesitates for a second, watching me closely trying to tell if I'm telling the truth or a lie.

"Truth," she finally says, and then she sinks down on top of me in one powerful stroke.

"Stingray!" I cry out, finally feeling the connectedness I need. I don't touch her like I want. I let her decide what I get to do. I'm just thankful to be connected to her in any way.

She doesn't move at first. She just lets the connection be only my cock inside her pussy. And for a moment, that's enough.

Our eyes hold, unspoken words pass between us.

She forgives me.

And I love her even more for it.

Then I'm grabbing her, and she's thrusting over me with everything she has. Our bodies connect in a wild fury. She grinds her body down on top of mine, and the love we share for each other flows freely between us, just like it has since the moment I realized I loved her. She is the missing piece of my life I thought I would never have.

She rides me like this is going to last forever, like we will never experience another moment after this one. This is the last instant that matters.

I watch my wife come undone on top of my cock. Her body changes from pain to love. Her eyes roll back, her hair falls freely down her back, her cheeks flush bright pink, her nipples harden, and her hips roll over mine as her orgasm approaches until she can't hold on anymore. She lets go.

I'm so lost in her that I don't realize my own body is coming right with her, exploding inside of her, giving her all of my cum.

Slowly we both stop—neither of us speak. We don't

have to after what just happened. Our bodies already did all of the talking. We love each other. We forgive each other. We would forgive each other for anything. That's how much we love each other. There was never a question about forgiveness or reconciliation. We were always going to end up loving each other forever.

"Come here," I say, pulling her against my chest.

She falls on top of me as my cock slips out of her. We are a mess. We should shower off the seawater, cum, blood, and sweat. But we won't.

Being clean right now doesn't matter.

I hold Kai against my chest. Her hand traces slowly over my heart.

"I love you, Stingray."

"I love you, too."

"What are you thinking?" I know her. Even though we just shared that incredible, mind-blowing moment together, she still has dozens of thoughts racing in her head.

"I'm still mad at Zeke. And unfortunately, I can't fuck him and make it all better."

My head swivels to her, and my hand grabs her hand, forcing her to stop tracing circles on my chest.

"Damn right, you can't fuck him," I growl.

She smiles. "I didn't mean I want to fuck Zeke. I just meant that making up with you is easier than making up with him."

Our fingers dance together as I hold her hand. I can feel her heartache from being angry at Zeke flow through her. It will eat at her until she can see him again, which is exactly what she doesn't need. She needs to be focused on protecting herself and this family.

"There is nothing to forgive," I say.

She leans on her elbow and sits up. "What do you

mean? He fucking shot you! He needs to crawl on his knees and beg for my forgiveness and hope I don't shoot him for what he did to you."

I smile, loving how far she would go for me. She just needs someone to blame for the fear she felt in the moments when she didn't know if the plan had worked or not.

"No, you have no reason to be angry with Zeke, and you know that. Zeke knew we were all wearing the bulletproof armor. He knew they would spurt fake blood, so our enemies thought the bullets were hitting us and not our protective gear.

"He knew that by shooting me himself that I was most likely helping him complete Julian's task. He knew that pushing me into the ocean was more about saving me than killing me. He knew. He knew that I would survive. He knew.

"He did it to protect me, to protect you, and get you the fuck off the boat and after me. He did it to protect Siren. What Zeke did doesn't need to be forgiven. What he did needs to be thanked. The only reason we are all here is because Zeke saved us."

Kai narrows her eyes, her lips jut out a little as she pouts adorably. She kisses me sweetly on the cheek.

"You're a good friend," she says before trying to pull away.

I yank her back. "And you're a better one. Don't hold this against Zeke. Not after everything you two have been through. Your friendship shouldn't change because of this."

She sighs but kisses me again before she tries to climb out of bed, again.

"Why do you keep trying to climb out of my bed, Stingray?"

"Because we need to go get to the box I hid before anyone else finds it."

I shake my head.

She folds her arms over her chest.

Both of us in a standoff position, ready to fight.

"We need to sleep. We can get the box in the morning."

"That's bullshit, and you know it. Julian could have already reached the box by now."

"Where did you hide it?"

She closes her mouth tighter like that will make it harder for her to spill the truth.

I can't help it. I laugh a little.

"We need to go, right now."

"No, we don't. We need to rest. We need all our strength to fight off Julian and his men. We've lost too many times already. I'm tired of losing."

She gnaws on her bottom lip, and I can see the worry lines forming around her eyes again. There is something she isn't telling me.

"Spill," I command.

She takes a deep breath. And I prepare for her to say something stupid.

"I hid the box in Alaska."

Fuck.

I jump out of bed so fast. In record time, we have both rinsed off, dressed, and are headed upstairs to tell the captain our new coordinates.

I love my wife. I know why she hid the box there. It's safest there. I just hope to God that Nora and Beckett didn't choose it as a place to hide our kids.

We are in this together, though. Together, we are going to stop this bastard, destroy the box, and keep our family safe.

5

ZEKE

I HEAR Julian's helicopter turning around and know I have limited time to get to Siren before he kills me.

I'm a sitting duck here in the ocean. There are no boats around. All the yachts that were here before have left, including the one Siren was on.

I don't know how well Julian can fly a helicopter, but my time is limited.

I start swimming in the direction I saw Siren's yacht go. I don't have a plan. There is nothing I can do but swim and hope it's enough.

The ocean has not always been my friend. Ultimately, it has never taken my life, and the ocean did bring me Siren. The ocean may be an obstacle, but as much as it has threatened my life, it has blessed it just as much.

I don't know what the ocean will choose this time. I don't know if I'll be able to get to Siren or if the ocean will finally take me.

As the buzz of the helicopter gets closer, I have a sinking feeling that the ocean is not going to be my friend. There is no one to save me. No one knows I'm here and is going to come back for me.

Kai has long ago found Enzo. And Siren is gone.

The helicopter gets closer. All I know is that I won't follow Julian's orders. I won't go back. I have to be free. It's the only way I have a chance at saving Siren from Langston.

As the helicopter approaches, I make a decision.

Ocean, now is the time to save me.

I take a deep breath.

Then I dive under.

I kick as far down as I can get my body to sink.

I stare up at the sky and watch the helicopter buzz around. I won't be able to survive down here long. I'll run out of oxygen soon, and then I'll have to surface. When I do, Julian will spot me.

As my oxygen evaporates, I scramble, looking for something, anything that can save me. A boat to come by. A floating piece of driftwood to hide under—something.

Instead, my foot tangles in a damn plastic bag. *Fucking people acting like the world is their garbage can and not throwing away their recycling properly.* I untangle my foot from the plastic and am about to kick for the surface when I spot something in the bag.

I realize the bag is a McDonald's takeout bag, and inside is a cup and a straw.

A straw!

I have no idea if it will work, but I'm willing to try anything to get Siren back safely. I was stupid to take Julian's deal. I should have known he would never honor it. He would send Langston to watch over Siren and somehow persuade him to eventually kill her.

I grab the straw and put it between my lips as I head for the surface. I'm careful to keep my body under the water, hoping that even though I'm at the surface, Julian can't see me. The straw sticks out above the waves, and I take a cautious breath.

It works.

I can breathe.

Albeit, in short, painful breaths—breaths that don't fully satisfy my lungs. Breaths half-filled with salt water as the waves bump into my straw. But breaths that keep me alive and hidden from view. Breaths that get me one step closer to helping Siren.

So I'll hover here, at the surface of the water, and wait until Julian has to head for shore to land. Then I'll surface. Then I'll swim all night, and the next night and the night after that, until I find land or a boat. I'll find Siren, and I'll kill everyone who threatens her life, even my ex-best friend, Langston.

Julian hovers for twenty minutes until he finally heads toward shore to land.

I break the surface, gasping and coughing hard, expelling the water that slowly entered my lungs with each breath. It takes a solid minute of coughing until I can breathe semi-normally again.

The ocean spared me.

But I still have a long way to go to get Siren back.

I start swimming, not thinking about how exhausted and tired I am already, not thinking about it being smarter to conserve energy and float here until a boat comes.

I swim like I'm Michael Phelps in an Olympic race.

I swim as hard and as fast as my arms and legs can move. I'm a big guy, but not in the way Phelps is. My wing-span is big, but more in a giant grizzly bear sort of way. My legs are more like tree trunks than flippers. But right now, if I were racing Phelps, I'd put money on me swimming faster.

Phelps never had to chase after the woman he loved to keep her safe before.

I swim all night, and when the sun rises, I have hope when I see a boat in the distance headed straight toward me.

It could be Julian's, but I don't have a choice but to get on it. So when the boat approaches and I wave it down, I climb up hesitantly. I don't have a gun on me. Physically, I'm in no shape to fight, but tell that to my heart.

When I hit the deck, I know the men are dangerous. They don't have their guns pointed at me, but I see the outlines of them beneath their clothes.

"You okay, man?" one man says.

"Yea, I could use a towel, though," I say.

The man nods and turns like he's going to go get me a towel. He doesn't get a step in before I've grabbed him by the neck, pulled his gun out, and aimed it at his head.

All the men tense. Some grab their guns and point it at me.

"I'm Zeke Kane. And I have no problem killing this man and every single one of you if I have to. My wife is in danger. I've survived an entire night chasing after her in the ocean, and no one is going to stop me. Now, put your guns down."

All the men immediately drop their guns to my surprise. Either they all love the man I'm pointing my gun at, or they are all pussies.

"Mr. Kane, we are at your service. We didn't recognize you at first, but we work for Kai Black. We will take you wherever you need and fight by your side," the man standing in front of me says.

I look around at all the eyes staring back and me. I recognize a few men and even know a few by name.

I found one of the Black organization's ships. *Thank God.*

I release the man I'm holding.

"I'll go get you that towel," the man says, scampering off.

I chuckle. I don't give a damn about a towel. I can stay dripping wet and cold. The only thing that will truly warm me is getting Siren back.

"Where to, sir?" Dustin, a man I recognize, says, looking at me for direction.

"I need to get to the security system," I say now that I recognize this as one of the Black's boats. We put a tracking system on all the yachts. We can track the one that Langston and Siren are on.

An hour later, we pull up to the shore of San Salvador Island. I spot the yacht parked at the end of the pier, and I don't wait until our boat is tied up to jump onto the pier and run to their boat.

"Siren!" I scream as I run to the yacht.

I don't get an answer. I pull my gun out in case I face Langston. I realize now why Siren wanted us all to shoot first as soon as we were faced with Bishop. She knew Bishop was Langston, our supposed friend. She knew but couldn't break our hearts. She warned us in the only way she knew how.

I failed before. I won't fail this time. If I come face to face with Langston again, I'll shoot him and ask questions later. That's what he deserves after what he did to Siren.

"Siren!" I yell as I run through the top deck.

Nothing.

I move up to the top decks.

Nothing.

I run down to the bottom decks and yell. I open every door slowly, through the painstaking security process that Kai and Enzo installed on their yachts so each room could act like a safe room when danger approached.

Nothing.

They aren't here.

I emerge and walk back onto the pier, where the men have now disembarked the boat.

"Did you find her?" Dustin asks.

"No, but they couldn't have gone far," I say, although my words are more of a hope than a truth.

Dustin nods. "We will canvass the town. We will find her, Mr. Kane."

"Call me Zeke."

"Of course."

"Let's go."

I don't bother putting the gun away. I don't give a fuck if the police try to arrest me, or if I'm putting fear into people around me. I need the gun to shoot Langston or Julian if I see either of them.

Most people don't notice the gun, or if they do, they don't question it. They look at me and feel like it belongs to me. And no one dares take it away.

I search the island, and everywhere I look, I see Siren. Every woman with long brown hair and a thin muscular frame must be her. But she's not here.

Where are you, baby? Call out to me. Use your voice. Tell me where you are.

If I can't find them in town, I'm guessing they went to the airport. I'm about to tell the men that's where I'm headed when I stop dead in my tracks.

Walking casually down the sidewalk like two friends are Siren and Langston. She is talking quickly, and he is shaking his head, which makes her laugh.

She's laughing.

I don't know how to process this scene. My brain expected to find her tied up with a knife or gun to her throat. I expected to find her hurt, hanging onto life, not walking downtown like she's headed to get a coffee or pick up a souvenir at one of the local shops.

What.

The.

Fuck.

I want to run across the street and grab her. I want to shoot Langston and beat him until he answers every question.

Instead, I watch. I try to understand what is happening. Why she is walking with him so calmly?

Maybe I was wrong? Maybe he isn't Bishop? I did tell her to trust him after all.

No.

Julian confirmed he was Bishop.

Langston is Bishop.

I'm about to shoot Langston when I hear the click of a gun behind me. I don't have to turn around to know who is standing behind me with a gun pointed at my head.

Julian Reed.

I was too focused on Siren. It gave him the opportunity to sneak up on me.

"Come with me or Siren dies," Julian says.

He's threatened our lives before, and every time I've fallen for it. I've not killed him because I thought it was the right thing to do. I thought the best way to protect Siren was to make a deal with Julian. Not anymore. Siren is pregnant. The only way to protect her and my baby is to kill the man behind me.

6

SIREN

I TAKE another step and try not to puke. Apparently, my morning sickness decided to kick in now, at the worst possible time. I'm stuck on a yacht with a man I have no idea if I should trust or not, while trying to avoid another madman who might kill me or my baby, while also trying to figure out how to save my husband from dying to protect me.

Perfect timing.

"Do you have what you need yet?" Langston Bishop asks next to me.

"No, I told you I need Sprite and crackers. That always helps when I feel sick."

He sighs. "You do realize that sugar water is not going to help you. It's crap."

I chuckle. "It will help me. It always helps."

He rolls his eyes. "Let's try this store. If they don't have it, though, we are buying what they have and getting the hell out of here."

He grabs my bicep and guides me into the fifth store we've entered on the island. I was surprised when I started puking last night that Langston changed course and directed us to the nearest island. He did it to get me medical help. I said I didn't need it, just Sprite and crackers.

"Look, they have 7-Up and oyster crackers," Langston says as he leads me to the back of the store.

I keep waiting for him to pull a gun on me, to lose his patience, and say he's done with my silly mission, but so far he hasn't. We just keep going from store to store, him humoring me like my mission is going to actually help me, when actually each store we enter is another chance for me to escape.

He knows that, but still, he allows me to do it.

I scrunch up my nose. "I said Sprite, not 7-Up."

"Isn't that the same thing?"

"No, it is most definitely not. Sprite is heaven from the gods. 7-Up is like dog piss."

Langston shakes his head. "I don't know how Zeke puts up with you. You are the most frustrating woman."

"If you don't want to put up with me, you could just let me go. I'll stay here and keep up my search for Sprite, while you can go look for the box that holds the weapon to take down the world in it."

"I think I spotted another store on the corner. Maybe they have your precious Sprite and crackers."

I frown, not understanding why he hasn't grabbed the supplies and marched my ass back on the boat.

But I can't think about that for long before my stomach is queasy again and I'm going to be sick in this cute seaside store, if I don't find a bathroom soon.

Langston springs into action. He picks me up honeymoon style and carries me to the bathroom before depositing me on the floor in front of a toilet, seconds before I'm sick.

I don't know at what point in me throwing up that he leaves, but when my stomach finally settles, I realize I'm alone in the bathroom. I walk to the sink and wash my hands before splashing water on my face and deciding that when I exit, I'll take the 7-Up.

When I leave the bathroom, I find Langston Bishop standing there.

"How you feeling?"

"Like death. I'll take the 7-Up."

It's then that Langston holds out the items in his hands —Sprite, crackers, and a bag of something else.

"You found Sprite?"

He nods with a smug smile.

I take the items from him and immediately start sipping on the Sprite. It feels like fizzy heaven going down my throat. I tear open the crackers and munch on them as well, instantly knowing that I'll be able to get through this now that I have the items I've been desperate for.

"What's that?" I ask about the bag.

"More crackers and Sprite. I made sure to stock up."

"Good thinking."

"And some ginger." He pulls the item out and offers it to me. "Munch on this, it will help more than that disgusting carbonated death drink."

"Hey, the Sprite is helping."

"Sure, it is. Just try it." I take the piece of dried ginger from his hand, and I pop it into my mouth, deciding I should be nice.

We walk out of the store with the items in hand.

"Better?" he asks as we walk.

I feel much better, so I nod.

He grins, thinking the ginger is helping. But it's definitely my Sprite.

Langston Bishop starts guiding me back toward the yacht.

"I'm not getting back on that thing with you. I have my Sprite, but it's not a miracle cure. It won't keep me from getting sick again."

"You're sick because you have morning sickness, not because of motion sickness from the yacht. Come on."

"No, I'm not going anywhere with you."

"You don't have a choice, Siren. Trust me."

I scoff, still munching on my crackers. "You want me to trust you?"

He nods.

"Then fix me. Fix what you did to my head. Make it so that I don't dream about you anymore. So that your words aren't in my head. Fix me. Earn my trust. Then maybe I'll go with you willingly."

He stops walking, so I do too. His eyes narrow, trying to read my thoughts to determine if he gives me what I want if I'll really work with him willingly. Doubtful. I just want him to fix me, so I can be free.

My head starts spinning the longer he looks at me. I feel him creeping back into my head, my thoughts...

Come with me.

Don't fight me.

Do what I say.

It's easier.

I shake it off and try to focus on the man in front of me, instead of the version of him who has been haunting me and demanding my thoughts.

We continue our stare-off. Neither of us budge or move. I hope like hell that Langston Bishop doesn't realize how much he can still control my thoughts, and that he can't tell how weak I am. How easily he can win.

"Come with me," he says.

"No," I say firmly, surprising myself when the word I'm thinking is yes.

"Fine."

Wait, did I just win?

Langston Bishop grabs my arm, and he's lifting me in his arms again.

Nope, I definitely didn't just win.

I fight. "Let me go! You can't just do whatever you want to me!"

"I told you to come with me. To get on the boat. You chose not to; your decision has consequences."

I beat against his chest as he climbs onto the yacht, but I don't struggle too much. I'm afraid he'll drop me and hurt the baby. He knows that. It's like fighting while handcuffed. I only have limited ways that I can fight.

But I am a fighter. I won't give up just because I'm pregnant, especially when this man thinks he can bully me around after doing horrendous things to me.

So while I'm yelling and beating against his chest, I'm also making a plan.

I search for his gun with my eyes. I find it. As soon as we are firmly on the deck of the ship, I grab it and then kick hard, forcing him to drop me. I'm prepared and land on my feet, aiming the gun at his head.

Langston doesn't react like I expect him to. He doesn't put his hands up. He's not afraid of death, not in the least. *Or is he not afraid of me?*

"Now, fix me. Tell me how to get you out of my head, or I'll shoot you."

"Shoot me."

"What?"

"Shoot me, it will make you feel better."

I frown. *Why does he want me to shoot him?* I glance over my shoulder, but there is no one behind me. We were the only ones on the yacht when we arrived, but I don't trust that he doesn't have other men here. That must be the real reason we stopped, not to get me my damn Sprite.

"No one is here. Shoot me, Siren."

I smirk. "If I shoot you, I'll kill you. I'm not some weak girl who has never held a gun before. This is what I do for a living. This is who I am. I shoot you, I kill you."

"You won't kill me."

"Yes, I will."

"No, because if you kill me, you'll never know the truth. You'll never know how to fix your head. I'll always be there, even when I'm gone."

Dammit. Dammit. Dammit.

Continuing to aim the gun at Langston Bishop, I'm more confused than ever who the man standing in front of me is. *Is there still a piece of him that is Zeke's old friend? Or is he all monster now?*

What should I do?

Shoot him.

Kill him.

Or surrender.

Surrendering doesn't seem like an option. Killing him isn't one either.

But I could shoot him. I could hurt him.

I could make him pay for everything he's done to me.

Would it really help?

It would make me feel a tiny bit better to know that I got a little piece of revenge. And maybe it would strike a tiny bit of fear into him.

I don't think.

I fire.

One single shot.

It hits him in the shoulder, just above his heart.

He doesn't react. He doesn't flinch. He doesn't reach for his shoulder. He stands there as solid as ever.

I frown, and my head drops to the side, annoyed. "You're wearing a bulletproof vest."

He grabs the back of his shirt and yanks it over his head. His abs ripple into my view. He's not wearing a vest. With the shirt off, I spot the bullet wound in his shoulder with blood dripping out.

"Now that you got that out of your system, go rest while I set sail. And eat more of the ginger," he says before storming away.

He doesn't wait to make sure I head toward a bedroom. He's not afraid of me running off. Letting me shoot him was another attempt at gaining my trust.

Fuck him.

I'm leaving. I'll find the box myself. I'll go after Zeke. I'll save the motherfucking world. And when I do, I'll come back and kill him.

"*LET ME GO TO HER FIRST,*" *Bishop says.*

"*Why? So you can fuck her first? I don't think so. I've waited a long time for this. She's mine," Julian says.*

"*Getting the information is more important than raping her. Let me talk to her.*"

"*You can talk after I have her.*"

I hear a loud sound.

"*You punched me, you bastard.*"

"*Don't touch her. Don't rape her. She doesn't deserve that.*"

. . .

I BLINK RAPIDLY. *Did that really happen? Or was that another dream?* Another thought Bishop put in my head.

My head is throbbing. I need to lie down.

The engines start up. I have limited time left to make my decision—jump now or stay with Langston Bishop on this yacht.

I watch the gap between the yacht and pier grow bigger until the space becomes too big to jump. If I jumped now, I'd end up in the water.

I choose to say. I need to rest. More importantly, I need answers...

7

ZEKE

I KNOCK the gun out of his hand in one swift motion. I get Julian in a headlock, intent on killing him, when I see Siren and Langston exit the building and start walking down the street.

I can't lose them. I need to get Siren. I need to make sure she's safe.

I raise my gun to finish Julian when Dustin rounds the corner. He looks at me holding Julian in a headlock.

"What do you need me to do?" he asks.

I should stay and make sure Julian's interrogated and then killed, but I have to be the one to ensure that Siren is alive and safe.

I want Julian Reed interrogated. I want to know everything he knows. I want to ensure there are no other people he's working with, but I want him dead more. Every second he's still alive is a second that he could escape and kill us.

I throw Julian into Dustin's capable arms.

"Kill him and then meet me at our yacht."

He nods.

Then I'm running out into the street, trying my best to

think that Julian is dead. That he won't escape this time. That it doesn't matter that I'm not the one to put the bullet in his head. I just need to keep Siren safe. That's what I do —protect. And protecting others doesn't mean that I have to be the one to kill him.

When I round the corner onto Main Street, I don't see Siren or Langston, but they couldn't have gone far. I scan quickly through the crowds of shoppers casually strolling down the sidewalks, through the cabs and cars honking at each other.

Where did they go?

My heart says the pier. I run down the street, and I see several more men who work for Black and were with me on the yacht.

"Go to the alley between Second and Third Avenues. Make sure that Dustin kills the man he's holding," I bark.

The men nod and run in that direction, while I continue on to the pier.

I spot the yacht at the end—it's moving.

"Fuck."

I run down the pier, moving as fast as humanly possible. And then I'm at the end of the pier. The yacht is still creeping along, but soon it will be in deep enough water that it can pick up speed.

I have two choices. Either get in my boat and chase after them again or jump in the water and swim.

I choose the latter, as they're not going very fast yet, and I need to be as quiet as possible.

I take a deep breath as I prepare to jump back in the water. "Fucking hell."

I jump back into the cool water. I hate this ocean right now, but it gives me a chance at saving Siren.

Their yacht continues to pull away as I swim, but there

is no way I'm letting it get away. I push my arms through the water and kick hard with my legs, ensuring that I swim as fast as humanly possible.

Catching up to them, I grab onto a loose floating buoy at the back of the yacht. I exhale a deep breath in relief. I'm not on the boat yet, but it won't get away from me, not this time.

Hand over hand, I pull myself up the rope until I can grip the railing of the boat. Then I pull myself out of the water and over the railing onto the deck of the yacht.

I'm huffing hard, my chest expanding and deflating wildly when I stand up. My body is fatigued, but I don't care. I don't know what danger is on this yacht. I don't know if it's just Siren and Langston or if Langston has more men on the boat, just like I do back at shore.

I should have called and had my men get on the yacht to meet me here, but I don't have time for even a phone call. I need to get Siren. I need to protect her. I need her in my arms.

And I need to kill Langston.

Fuck, I can't think about that. That's going to wreck me, no matter what he did to Siren. Shooting Enzo was bad enough even though Kai eventually got word to me that he's alive after making me suffer first.

Although, I just now realize that his bitchass has all my money since I had to buy Siren from him. That will make it easier to shoot him.

I pull my gun out as I creep through the yacht.

It's eerily quiet.

Someone is obviously steering the yacht, but that is one of the most secure rooms in the yacht. If it's locked, I'm not getting in. Hopefully, that's not where Siren is.

I make it to the stairs where I have to decide. *Do I go up or down?*

Downstairs are bedrooms with locks that I will have to manually unlock. If Siren is downstairs, she's most likely tied up and locked away.

Something tells me to go up, even though it makes no sense to me.

I keep my gun pointed in front of me as I climb the stairs, not having a clue what I'm going to find.

When I reach the top deck, the wind of the yacht speeding up brushes though me, but that's not what takes my breath away.

Siren.

She's leaning against the railing as the sun beats down on her. She's wearing tiny shorts and a flowy tank-top that hides her growing belly. She looks like sunshine in the middle of the darkest storm.

The second both of my feet are on deck, Siren turns and faces me. For a second, we just stand, not sure what we are seeing is real. We only just saw each other last night. It's been less than twenty-four hours since we've been apart, but it feels like a lifetime.

I said goodbye to her. I thought I was going to die, or even if I did survive, I would do such horrible atrocities to protect my family that she would never want me. I thought I was leaving her with the best person possible. I couldn't have been more wrong.

"I'm really here," I say when tears water her eyes.

Then we are running at each other like we haven't seen each other in years.

I grab her in my arms before we collide too hard. I don't want to hurt the baby, but I can't help but spin her around a second before I kiss her hard on the lips. My joy at seeing her safe and kissing her again overtakes all other feelings.

"You're here. How? Why? How?" Siren starts.

"Shh," I say before kissing her again. Langston must be on the bridge, but I don't know for how long. Once we are out to sea, he can set the autopilot and come search for her.

"We need to go," I say.

"Go?" Her eyes dart out to the ocean. She's right. We aren't going anywhere. I might brave the seas and swim the mile to shore, but I would never allow Siren to. And as we pick up speed, that option becomes less than ideal.

"I need to get you somewhere safe; then I can deal with Langston."

She laughs, not the reaction I was expecting.

"Oh, so you're going to tell me your plan this time before you leave me somewhere safe? Not like last time where you left me with the enemy and didn't let me talk about the plan first."

I frown. She's right, but I don't care right now. I just want her safe.

"Are Enzo and Kai safe? Alive?"

"Yes," I say.

"What about Julian?"

I suck in a breath. "Dead."

She narrows her eyes. "What does that mean?"

"It means he's dead."

"You're lying. Why?"

I bite my lip as my veins pop out of my head and blood swishes through my body like raging rivers. "Because I had him. I could have killed him, but instead, I came after you. I needed to know that you were safe."

"So, why do you think he's dead?"

"Because men who work for Kai and Enzo found me.

They are working for me. They ran into me when I got Julian. I told them to kill him."

We both stare at each other. Julian Reed could be dead. Or he could have escaped again.

"He's not dead," we both say at the same time.

"At least we need to assume he's not dead until we know for sure," Siren says.

I nod reluctantly.

"I think I'm going to be sick." Siren grabs at her stomach. "Can you help me to a bathroom?"

I take her hand. I want off this boat immediately, but I'll go along with what she wants. And we don't have another option at the moment. She'll be safe enough in one of the bedrooms with me as her guard.

I hold my gun in one hand as I lead her down, hoping like hell that Langston doesn't pop out, and I don't have to shoot him. I've shot enough of my friends to last me a lifetime.

When we make it into one of the bedrooms, I quickly lock the door, praying Langston hasn't overridden the security system already. I help Siren to the bathroom just before she vomits.

I rub her back, hold her hair, anything I can do, but I don't feel like I'm doing enough.

Finally, she sits back.

"I need my Sprite."

I frown. *Sprite?*

"Is there some up in the kitchen?"

"No, it's in the bag on the bed."

I get up and return with the bag and hand her a Sprite. Then I pull out crackers and ginger.

"You should really try the ginger. It would help."

She rolls her eyes. "Don't get me started."

I sit next to her on the bathroom floor, as it doesn't look like we are leaving anytime soon. I still hold the gun, but Langston hasn't come searching for her, so I have no idea if he knows I'm here or not.

"How did you get these supplies anyway?"

"That's why we stopped at the island. I was getting sick and said I needed them. Langston agreed to stop." She nibbles at the corner of a cracker as she looks at me.

"Why would he do that?"

She raises her shoulders.

I frown, staring at my hands that are folded above my knees with my gun in my hand. "I should call my men, tell them to meet the yacht, and then attack."

"No."

"Why not?"

"Because I need Langston Bishop to trust me."

"Langston Bishop? You know Bishop isn't his last name, right?"

"I know, but until I figure out who he is, I call him by both names."

"He's Langston, the monster who tortured you."

She's quiet.

"What aren't you telling me?"

"I'm just not sure about him. I'm not sure I remember correctly what he did to me."

"What do you mean?"

"I mean that he may or may not have tortured me."

"That's pretty black and white. How do you not know?"

She stands up suddenly. I follow as she walks into the bedroom and begins to pace. "My head is all fucked up. I don't know what he did. The memories I do remember are clouded. They keep coming back to me in short bursts that don't make sense."

"Which is why we need to leave, now."

"No, I need Langston to fix me."

"He won't. He's too far gone. He's evil now."

She raises her eyebrows. "Don't you start. By that measure, we are both evil, too."

I take her hand and place it over her stomach. "We are."

She smiles.

"That's why we have to destroy our enemies—to protect this little guy."

"Guy, huh?"

I shrug. "Our little warrior."

"Better."

I keep my hand on her stomach.

"Langston Bishop trusts me. I think he does, or he wants me to trust him. And I think I can trick him into fixing me, by guaranteeing I'll work with him if he fixes me."

"No."

"We don't have a choice. I can't live with him in my head. It's not safe for our little warrior. I've had thoughts, dark thoughts. I'm afraid I'll go crazy."

Fuck.

"What do you suggest then?" I say.

"Langston Bishop doesn't know you are here. You stay hidden and prepared to protect me, while I convince him to fix me. It's the safest plan."

"I don't like it."

"You don't have a choice."

"Fine, but if he puts one hand on you, I'll kill him."

She nods, agreeing.

"I'll sneak into the security room and get it wired so I can watch the feed on my phone. Then I'll stay hidden but close so I can protect you. I won't let him hurt you. I promise."

"I need to go check on him."

"Check on him? Why? Won't he come find you?"

She bites her lip as a blush spreads. "Probably not."

"Why not?"

She kisses me once more on the lips, and as much as I want to fuck her right here, she was just sick and needs to go deal with Langston. The sooner she can convince him, the sooner she'll be safe.

"He's been shot and is probably in need of stitches. I'm guessing once he set the autopilot, he either took a pain pill or alcohol to pass out from the pain."

"Who shot him?"

Siren walks to the door and opens it with a grin. "Me."

I smile back as I follow her out to head to the security room. "That's my girl," I whisper in her ear before kissing her hair and disappearing into the shadows.

She doesn't need me to protect her, but I'll be here, waiting in the shadows. Waiting for the moment when I can finally save her for good.

8

SIREN

I walk up the stairs, feeling Zeke behind me in the hallway. With each step I take, I feel Zeke's presence less and less. I don't know if I'm making the right decision. I don't know if convincing Langston to trust me is a good move or not. Or if I should just have Zeke kill him, as horrible as that sounds.

Right now, all I can focus on is putting one foot in front of the other. It's an impossible task as it means each step I take is further away from Zeke.

"I'll be watching you. I'm with you. You got this," Zeke says from behind me.

His words feed me. I take another step, then another. Then I'm on the upper deck. Zeke is no longer with me, but he'll be watching from the security cameras.

I'm safe.

I rub my stomach. *We're safe.*

I head to the bridge and knock on the door.

There is silence at first, but then I hear the door unlocking and crack open. I push my way inside.

I find Langston Bishop shirtless as he holds some gauze

to his shoulder where I shot him. There is an open first-aid kit lying on the counter next to where he sits staring out at the ocean out the front window.

I smile; I can't help it. He looks young and innocent as he fumbles with the supplies trying to pull out the tweezers.

"Your stomach better?" he asks.

I nod.

"Good."

He removes the gauze from his wound without a drop of pain on his face. Then he begins digging into his wound to pull out the bullet fragment. He starts to pull something out, but it's not the bullet, instead, it's pieces of his flesh.

"Fuck," he curses under his breath. I don't think it's from the pain, just the frustration of not being able to find the bullet.

"Need some help?"

He ignores me and digs the tweezers in. Again, he comes up empty.

I sigh. I can't watch him struggle.

I march over and grab the tweezers from his hand, dig them into his wound, and pull out the bullet. I drop it into the trash bin.

I don't bother asking if he needs additional help. I just go to work. I swab the wound with alcohol and then find a staple gun that I can use instead of doing the stitching by hand.

"Do you need any pain medication or alcohol first?" I hold the staple gun up, letting him know what I'm about to do.

He grunts.

"I'll take that as a no."

I start stapling.

"So considerate of you to ask if I need pain medicine before you staple me up, but not before you shoot me."

"You told me to shoot you!" I insert another staple. This time he hisses.

"So you can feel pain. I thought you might be immune to feeling anything," I say smugly.

He rolls his eyes. "Of course, I can feel pain. But there is no use reacting to it; it doesn't make the pain go away. It doesn't make it any better."

"I agree," I say as I put the last staple into his arm.

Our eyes meet in a weird moment of understanding each other. I don't know what happened to Langston that turned him into Bishop. I don't know what pain he felt or horror he experienced, but I can understand how someone can let pain turn to anger. Although, Langston doesn't seem angry.

I finish working on his arm, adding more gauze and then wrapping it around his arm to hold it in place.

"Thanks," Langston Bishop says suddenly.

I freeze. I wasn't expecting a thank you. Julian sure wouldn't say thank you after I stitched him up. He would have expected me to like I was his private nurse.

"You're welcome. Thanks for letting me shoot you. I feel better."

"Anytime," he says with a smile as he wiggles his eyebrows.

I laugh. "Really? I can shoot you anytime?"

He shrugs. "If you really need it. A bullet wound in an extremity is hardly anything unusual for me."

I let my eyes roam his chest for the first time, and it's then that I notice all the scars. Similar to Zeke's. Similar to mine.

I move the tank top straps on my shoulder, where I also wear the scar from a bullet wound.

He stares at it a moment. "We are more similar than we are different."

"Probably. But I didn't torture you. I just shot you after you told me to."

"You would have if given the chance." Langston closes the first-aid kit and puts it back on the wall.

"Of course."

He smiles at that and then moves back to the helm, looking at a navigation screen.

I consider asking him to fix me, or to take me home, but what truly matters right now is gaining his trust. I earned some of it by fixing his shoulder, but I need to use this moment to get more. I need something to continue the trust that is slowly building between us.

"Where are we going?"

His head turns to me, and I can see all of his thoughts turning behind his bright blue eyes. Between his eyes and blonde hair, he seems like light instead of the darkness toiling beneath the surface. It's the same darkness I feel inside Julian, yet it's different somehow.

"Spain," he answers.

My eyebrows raise, surprised he told me and not afraid to hide my shock to him.

"I have a house there. We need to put some distance between us and everyone else."

"Is that where the box is?"

He shakes his head.

"Then why are we going there?"

"We need some time and space for us to figure out where the box is."

His words tell me hardly anything, and yet they seem

important, like a hidden message hides in his words only I can decode. Except I don't have the code key.

I don't have a clue how to interpret his words or why we need time and space to find the box, when to my knowledge, Kai Black is the only person who knows where the box is because she hid it.

"Go get some rest. And try not to get sick. The Sprite we have has to last you all the way to Spain." He winks at me.

"You're not worried I'll escape between now and then?"

"How are you going to escape? We are in the middle of the ocean. We are all alone, just the two of us. I'll make sure we can't be tracked before I go to sleep."

"You can do that?"

"I helped build the security system. I know how to disable the tracker. And I know how to use the system to keep an eye on you."

"So sure of yourself."

He nods. "Go to bed. You aren't going anywhere. We both know that. You won't go anywhere for the same reason you won't kill me."

"Goodnight, Langston Bishop."

He frowns as I say the name I've been calling him in my head.

"Goodnight, Siren Kane." He uses Zeke's last name, and it warms my heart.

I head downstairs, anxious to talk to Zeke and to verify he's really here. I pray he hasn't left me, or that I didn't imagine him earlier.

I don't feel unsafe anymore around Langston Bishop, but I don't feel safe either. I feel on edge. I feel unbalanced. And I can't understand why.

I open the door to my room and look around. The room seems empty, except for the bed. I don't feel Zeke's presence.

I frantically move around the room, hoping he's come back from the security room before Langston Bishop headed there himself. I move to the bathroom but don't find him there either.

My shoulders slump. My heart squeezes. I need my husband. I need him, and I don't know how to call him back to me.

I lean against the counter in the bathroom, exhausted and anxious. If he comes face to face with Langston Bishop alone, Zeke will try and kill him, which will ruin everything. Zeke won't be able to forgive himself if he kills his friend without understanding his motives first. He won't forgive himself if my head never heals.

"Looking for someone?" Zeke says from the doorway.

I catch my breath seeing him here.

"Don't do that to me," I say as I race into his open embrace. His arms fall around my back, and he holds me tight against his chest.

"You're the one making me. If it were up to me, I'd shoot Langston now, and we could get off this yacht."

"How about you fuck me instead?"

9

ZEKE

HOW ABOUT YOU fuck me instead?

My body instantly hardens at her words. I'm so desperate for her. I need her. I need to fuck her. I need to feel connected to her in every way.

I feel selfish for wanting that when she's been sick and having to deal with Langston, while I hide like a silent bodyguard. Watching her help Langston while he stood shirtless in front of her drove me mad.

If we are going to keep this up, he better keep a shirt on from now on, because I won't survive otherwise.

And now she wants to fuck.

"I need you, Zeke."

"You have no idea what that does to me."

She smirks. "I have an idea." Her hand pushes between us until she's gripping my hardening cock.

"What about the security system? Are there cameras in the bedrooms?"

"No."

Siren smiles. "Lock the door then."

"Already done."

She lifts her arms and steps back, waiting for me to lift her shirt with a seductive bat of her eyelashes.

So I do as I'm silently told, and I'm rewarded by the most beautiful sight of her naked stomach and breasts. Siren has always been strong and muscular, but still very feminine. Now where her muscles once were flush against the surface is a softening, growing belly bump.

"I've never seen a more beautiful sight."

She blushes. "Take off my shorts."

I step forward. The button on her shorts is already unbuttoned. Soon her clothes won't fit over her stomach at all. I unzip the zipper and shimmy her shorts and underwear off her body until she is completely naked.

I'm speechless watching her.

"Your turn," Siren says as I stand in front of her, still completely clothed.

"Get in bed," I order.

Siren frowns.

"Bed," I command.

She pouts but does as I say, brushing past me and swaying her hips as she does. She's begging me to follow her with her body, but she doesn't need to beg; I'll be coming willingly.

I remove my clothes quickly and then turn off the lights before I walk to the bed. Siren is lying on top of the covers, her legs spread, her nipples pebbling for me.

"Under the covers," I command.

She frowns, thinking I'm turning her down. I'm not. I just don't want to fuck her. I want to love her like she's the queen. And if I touch her before getting her into bed where I want her, I'll lose my control and fuck her like an animal.

Once Siren is under the covers, I slide in next to her.

"Face the window."

Again she gives me a dirty look but rolls on her side.

I take a deep calming breath, trying my best not to let my need for her overtake me and turn into a devouring monster. I put my hand on her back, trailing my fingers down her spine slowly.

I watch her breath speed up at the gentle gesture. I add my heated breath, too, as I continue to trace her spine with my fingertips.

"Zeke," she breathes, her voice achy and needy.

I know what she wants. I'll give it to her, but first, she needs to relax. She needs to feel safe and loved. And I want this to last as long as it can, which means taking things excruciatingly slowly.

She takes a deep, calming breath. Her shoulders slump. I want her as relaxed as possible. I'm tired of making her tense and anxious. I'm tired of putting her through all of this. This needs to end. I need to stop this.

For now, the only thing I can help ease is her stress. Soon I will ensure that our enemies are gone, no matter the cost. No matter what I have to do, I will protect her and our baby.

My hands grip her neck, rubbing gently, then I move down to her shoulders and back, massaging every tense muscle. My hands slide lower, over her ass. I massage her ass too, then down her legs.

She moans, her back relaxing into my hands as I massage her back.

"Zeke," her voice grows more desperate.

"Shh, just feel. Don't think. Don't worry. I've got you."

Her head rolls back against my shoulder, and her arm reaches back, trying to pull me closer to her.

I grin, watching how relaxed, yet needy, she is.

Who am I kidding? I can't hold back much longer, either.

I push my body flush to hers until I can feel all of her back against my front. My cock pushes between her legs as I reach around and tease her nipples and kiss her neck.

"I love you. I want to protect you," I whisper.

She moans as I flick her nipple with my thumb.

"Let me protect you. Let me find a way to be the one to put myself in harm's danger, not you. I can't stand it. I love you too much to ever lose you. I wouldn't survive."

She takes my hand in hers, as her legs part and my cock slips closer to her entrance.

"Just like I couldn't lose you. It's not fair to think that you would be the only one to lose something if either of us fails," she says.

I push my hips forward slowly, so close to being inside of her, but knowing I won't last the second I am.

"Promise me you'll let me protect you."

She moans. "Promise me you won't risk your life to protect mine."

I can't promise any more than she can.

I reach between her legs and tease her clit.

"Promise me," I say, teasing her more, my cock taunting her entrance but not pushing inside her like she's begging.

She moans.

Neither of us can stand it anymore. I start thrusting inside her, giving her all that I have—all my dreams, desires, wants. I slide in and out, our bodies gliding together.

And just like I knew we would, too quickly we come.

We both muffle our cries. The rooms are soundproof, but it's still hard not to want to quiet our moaning when we don't want Langston to know.

I kiss over her ear, knowing she will never promise to let me protect her, but I'm going to promise her anyway. She needs to know how far I'll go, what I'll do to protect her. When she's scared or worried, she needs to know that she is safe. I will never let anyone hurt her again.

"I promise I'll protect you." I put my hand on her stomach. "I'll protect both of you—always."

10

SIREN

I'll always protect you.

Always.

Those words play over and over in my head as I fall to sleep.

You're safe.

I'll protect you.

I'll keep you safe.

Zeke?

No, it's not Zeke. He can't keep you safe. I can.

I sit up abruptly as memories start flooding my head. I gasp hard and fast, unable to catch my breath. My lungs are burning, and my chest is tight, but I don't feel it, not really. I'm too focused on trying to remember the fleeting images.

Zeke sits up abruptly next to me, grabbing his gun before he realizes how flushed I am. He puts his hand on my forehead.

"You're burning up," Zeke says, trying to hide the worry in his voice, but I can sense it all the same.

He runs to the bathroom and returns a minute later with a cool washcloth, a glass of water, and a thermometer.

He puts the thermometer in my mouth, giving me a few more seconds before I will have to speak.

Who was the man?

The thermometer beeps, and Zeke removes it from my mouth with a slight relaxation of his facial muscles. "No fever."

He shoves the water into my hand. "Drink."

I sip, but I'm not worried about having a temperature or an illness.

"A nightmare?" Zeke asks.

I take another sip and then hand Zeke the water.

"More like a memory."

"A bad one?" Zeke's forehead brows until lines form around his eyes.

"No."

Zeke rubs my back, helping me relax.

"Want to tell me what it was about?"

"Just a man telling me that he'll protect me, but it wasn't you."

Zeke frowns. "Enzo?"

"No, I don't know who the man was. He didn't have a face, and he didn't have a voice I recognized. At least the memory didn't."

A knock on the door startles us both.

"Langston Bishop," I say as Zeke aims his gun at the door.

Zeke sighs. "I don't want to leave you. Not until I'm sure you are okay."

"I'm fine." I stand up and head to the closet. I pull on a T-shirt and shorts and throw a robe over my body to stay warm.

Zeke is dressed but otherwise sitting on the edge of the bed.

"Hide," I hiss at him.

He frowns but eventually heads to the closet.

I open the door and find Langston standing in the doorway.

"What would you like for breakfast?"

I frown at him as I tuck the robe tighter around my body.

"Breakfast. Are you an eggs and toast kind of girl? Pancakes? Oatmeal?"

I continue to stare at him. I don't understand this man.

"Siren?" He waves his hand in front of my face.

"Sorry, um...oatmeal."

He nods. "I'll fix it. Do you want to eat upstairs or in your room?"

I want to eat here with Zeke, but something tells me I need to spend as much time as I can with Langston Bishop before we get to Spain. We need intel to decide on a plan. *Do I continue to go with him? Or do I let Zeke kill him?*

"I'll come up," I say.

His eyes dilate in slight surprise, but then he's gone.

"You should have eaten here," Zeke says from behind me.

"I need to figure out why he did what he did to me. Why I'm here. Is he still working with Julian? Is he more evil than good? Something happened, and I'm the only one he might talk to."

Zeke cracks his knuckles. "He'd talk to me."

"Yea, and then you might kill a man you shouldn't."

"There is no excuse for what he did to you." He tucks a loose strand behind my ear.

"There is more to Langston Bishop than you realize. I just have to figure him out."

I kiss him tenderly. "I'll be back. And I'll make sure to sneak you some food."

"Don't worry about the food. I'll sneak some. Just make sure Langston keeps his shirt on."

"What fun is that?" I tease.

Zeke frowns. "Not funny."

"I might just have to shoot him again to see those rippling abs."

Then I disappear out the door, preventing Zeke from saying anything back without chancing that Langston will hear him. I assumed wrong.

Zeke follows me out. He catches my hand before I make it to the stairs and then pulls me back to him.

Zeke, I mouth, motioning my head upstairs. Langston could come down any second, and I'd ruin all the trust I've built with him so far.

Zeke presses his lips hard to my mouth, capturing me and reminding me who I belong to. Like that is even a question.

I belong to Zeke. I always have. I always will.

I promise, I mouth to Zeke when we finally break the kiss. I run up the stairs knowing Zeke will be protecting me nearby while I figure out what is going on with Langston.

I spot Langston putting a bowl of oatmeal and an orange juice at a table, and my nerves catch up to me. *What am I doing with this monster? A man who has hurt me? A man who threatened my life?*

However, he didn't rape me when he could have.

He tried to stop Julian.

And he's been nice ever since I've been on this boat.

"Anything else you need?" he asks like he's about to leave.

I walk over to my table and sit down. "Are you not going to join me?"

"Do you want me to join you?"

"No, but then again, I would prefer not to be your captive in the first place. But since we are both here, I think it's best we make the most of this and talk to each other."

He sits down in front of me, and I'm surprised that he also has oatmeal in his bowl.

"Is oatmeal what you usually eat?" I ask, staring at him.

"No."

"Then why are you eating it?"

"Because that's what you wanted, and I didn't want to cook two things."

I smile.

I can see why Langston Bishop and Zeke used to be friends. There are a lot of similarities between them. *But what changed? What happened that threw him down this path so far diverged from Zeke's own path?*

"Tell me a story about you and Zeke," I say before I take a bite of my oatmeal like we are two friends reminiscing about the good ole days.

"No." He shoves a bite into his mouth.

"Why not? How much longer do we have until we get to Spain? Another week at least? Why not make the most of it?"

Langston Bishop puts his spoon down. "You aren't asking to pass the time."

My heart stills. He knows Zeke is here. I grip my spoon tighter; maybe I could somehow use it as a weapon if I needed to.

He stands up. "You're asking because you think I'm a good person, and you think you will be able to manipulate me by talking."

I stand up too. "I think there is more than the evil I saw when you first bought me. There is more to you. The old you is still there."

He looks at me gravely. "I'm not a good person, Siren. I never was. Stop trying to find that part of me."

I step in front of him, so he will have to physically move me if he wants to leave the kitchen. It's probably not a smart move, but in order to figure out what his motives are, I need to push him to his limits.

"Are you going to kill me?" I ask.

He doesn't answer. "Move, Siren. I don't want to play games with you."

I smile thinly. "You're a good person, Langston Bishop."

"Why do you say that?"

I move out of his way. "Because you aren't going to kill me."

"I never answered you when you asked that."

"Exactly. If I had asked Julian Reed that he would have answered yes immediately. You clearly have no plan of killing me."

Langston Bishop leans toward me, giving me his most menacing snarl. "Maybe I'm just not as obvious as Julian Reed."

I step aside, and then he leaves me standing in the kitchen.

I cross my arms and huff in frustration.

A few seconds later, Zeke appears. He grabs Langston's uneaten bowl of oatmeal and scarfs it down.

"What do you think?" I ask Zeke.

"I think you should stop this whole thing and let me go take him out."

I return to the table and take another bite of my oatmeal. I'm not hungry, but I know the baby needs food.

"What do you really think about him?"

Zeke looks out the door where Langston left. "I think I never knew my best friend at all." He doesn't look at me when he continues. "But I think we need to find out his motivations. I think we need to convince him to fix you. I think we need answers."

I kiss Zeke on the lips, knowing how hard it is for him to stand by and watch me try to manipulate his friend. It's tearing him up inside to watch me put myself in danger when he could easily get rid of the threat, even if it meant we would have to face bigger threats down the road.

I take both of our bowls to the sink and rinse them out, rinsing down the evidence of Zeke's presence.

"Where is he?" I ask Zeke.

He stares down at his phone that has the security feed on it. "The gym."

I crack my neck. "I could use a workout."

11

ZEKE

EVERY TIME I let Siren go back with Langston, I feel sick. My stomach knots, my chest tightens, my heart races. I'm sweaty and clammy, anxiety rising in my throat. My body reacts to the danger with a full-blown anxiety attack.

Even though I can protect Siren, save her in a moment, I'm sick because I'm the reason she's in this situation in the first place. If it wasn't for me, she would be safe. She wouldn't know who Langston is. She wouldn't have been tortured by him.

This is all my fault. She shouldn't be the one to fix the problem. I should. But Langston is talking to her. Slowly, and painfully. She can get him to talk without shedding any blood.

If I did this my way, Langston would be dead before he spoke a word.

Siren heads to the gym, where Langston is lifting weights in front of a mirror.

I stand outside the gym door. I caught the door at the last second to keep it from closing so I can listen through the door and watch on the screen as Siren enters the gym.

At first, she just walks over to Langston but doesn't say anything. She picks up some dumbbells and starts lifting them next to Langston like he isn't there.

Of course, they fall into sync, lifting the dumbbells up to their shoulders at the same time.

Jesus, I'm not going to survive this. I'm giving her until we get to Spain. That's it. Then this ends.

Langston's shirt comes off, and I almost come unglued. I want to break through the door, but I stop myself.

"Really? You can't workout with a shirt on?" Siren asks, rolling her eyes at him.

"I didn't ask you to join me. You were the one that followed me, remember?" Langston says.

"And you are the bastard who took her memories from her," I say, quietly to myself.

She throws her dumbbells down on the floor in frustration. "I'm not the one holding me captive here."

Langston watches her silently as she walks over to the boxing ring and starts putting on some gloves.

"What are you doing?"

"Punching you, so I don't shoot you again." Siren continues to strap the gloves onto her hands as Langston climbs into the ring.

"Punch away," he says, holding his arms out like he is just going to stand there and let him hit her.

Siren grins slyly, and then she throws a punch. Langston steps out of her way. He's the fastest of all of us. She's fought Enzo and me, and we all fight differently. I use my brute strength. Enzo uses a combination of speed and strength. Langston uses his speed and brains. He outsmarts his competitor. She's going to have to change her strategy if she wants to land a punch because he's too quick to be hit.

"Good, I thought you were just going to stand there and

let me punch you. If that was the case, I could have just as easily hit a punching bag," Siren says.

Langston smirks. "You won't hit me. Not without me blocking you."

"I shot you, didn't I?"

"Yea, that required zero skill. This requires a lot."

She throws another punch. It's slow on purpose to trick Langston into thinking she's slower than she actually is.

I grin. I know how well they both fight, but my money is on my girl.

As much as it puts me on edge that she is fighting while pregnant, I've seen her do it before and be fine. For some reason, Langston isn't fighting back, just dodging or blocking her punches.

"You're going to have to do better than that," Langston says.

Siren throws another punch, barely missing Langston's nose. "You mean, like that?"

Langston shoots her a dubious look. "I look forward to the day when we can fight fair. You have me at a disadvantage since I won't fight a pregnant woman."

Siren swings again. "And why is that? Julian would have no problem fighting me in my condition."

Langston's feet dance as he moves out of the way once again with a frown on his face. His muscles tense, and for once, I'm glad his shirt is off. It gives more clues as to what he's thinking.

"Come on, if you think this is so unfair, fight back," Siren goads him.

I tense, not liking this. If she succeeds in getting him to fight back, I might not be able to move fast enough to stop him from making contact.

"You're a good person, that's why," Siren says.

Langston grinds his teeth together. His muscles turn into a brick wall, and I think she's going to be able to make an impact now.

But she swings, he dodges.

"Why am I here? Why me?" Siren pleads as she swings in rapid succession.

"Why do you work for Julian when you hate him? I remember the hate in your voice when you were together. I remember you pleading him not to rape me. You tried to save me. You did everything you could."

More swings, more dodging.

"Why is that? You care about us? You care about your friends?"

Swing.

Dodge.

"What made you pretend to be someone you're not? Was it a girl?"

Swing, dodge; this one closer than all the rest. So close she actually brushed her glove against his cheek.

"Liesel? Is that the girl that broke your heart? Turned you evil?"

She struck a nerve, and this time when she punches, she hits him square in the jaw. She doesn't let up. She keeps punching him in the face again and again. She suddenly kicks hard to his stomach, bringing him to his knees.

Langston never retaliates, no matter how angry he gets. He won't hurt her, even though he's hurt her before. *What am I missing? What happened? What changed from before?*

She kicks again, and this time, her ankle seems to twist as she kicks, and she grabs her stomach.

She moans loudly and falls to the floor. I start to run through the door, scared to death something happened. She's in pain; maybe she lost the baby.

But as she falls, she looks into the corner of the room where the security camera is and winks. That wink is the only thing that keeps me back, reminding me this is a game to get Langston to tell us the truth.

Langston runs to her. "Are you okay? Is it the baby?"

"I don't know; my stomach," Siren cries dramatically, too dramatically. I know her well. Langston doesn't. He buys the lie.

Langston sits over her, worry filling his eyes. "I'll redirect us toward the nearest hospital, put out a mayday call, and see if there is a boat with a doctor nearby."

Siren smiles at his reaction.

"What?" Langston practically yells his worry in her face.

"Why are you worried about me? Why are you trying to protect me?"

"You're not really hurt. The baby's fine?" He falls back on his heels.

"Yes, the baby's fine. I'm fine. I played you to show you how much you care about me."

Langston sits down next to her. He stares at the floor and then finally up at her.

"I protect you because you are the only one who knows the location of the box. Your memories hold the key to finding it," Langston says.

Siren looks at him with confusion. "That's not possible. Zeke put the box in the vault. And then Kai moved it. She is the only one who knows, not me."

Langston is shaking his head, and my phone buzzes in my hand, and my view of the security cameras vanishes.

"It's a fake," he tells her.

My phone screen updates to show an incoming call—Kai.

Something tells me that I need to answer the phone. Kai wouldn't be calling me otherwise.

"Hello," I whisper as I step away from the door.

"We have a problem," Kai says, not bothering with pleasantries.

"I think I know."

"The box I hid isn't the real one. I opened it to destroy it. There was nothing in it."

I stare at the door, realizing there is so much I don't know.

"We have to find it. If it gets into Julian's hands—"

"He won't get it."

"How do you know?"

"Because Siren is the only person who knows where it is."

12

SIREN

My memories.

I'm the only one who knows where the box is.

None of this makes any sense.

I continue to stare at Langston Bishop, more confused than ever.

"Maybe we should make some tea or get you another Sprite; then I'll explain everything," he says.

"Tea would be nice."

He stands and then holds out his hand to help me up.

"And put a shirt on."

"Why? Am I too distracting?"

"No, but I'm married, and it's weird to be around you without a shirt on."

He pauses for a second; maybe I gave away that Zeke is here. Instead, Langston walks over to his shirt and puts it on. We walk back upstairs to the kitchen.

I try to force my brain to remember what Langston Bishop thinks I know, but all it does is give me a headache while Langston makes two cups of tea.

"Don't do that," he says. He carries the cups outside, and

we sit, looking out at the ocean. He hands me my cup, and I take it mindlessly.

"Don't do what?"

"Force yourself to remember. It's not good for you."

I stare at him incredulously. My heart beats rapidly, realizing how much I might be connected to him.

"Tell me the truth," I say.

"The box in the vault is fake."

"It's not in the vault anymore. Kai hid it."

"Well, wherever it is, it's fake."

"How?"

"Your parents and Julian's parents worked together."

I gasp. "No, there is no way. My parents were missionaries. They were religious and not always kind to me, but they would have no reason to be involved in something like this."

Langston sighs. "They wanted to rid the world of its evil with the viral cancer, and only use the cure on those they deemed worthy. Those who hadn't sinned."

I freeze, remembering their conversations. It sounds like them.

"Julian's parents felt much the same. Julian's mother worked with Lucy's mother in a lab in Miami. She realized what Lucy's mother had discovered, but it was too late to steal. Lucy had already given it to Zeke to hide. The vault was too hard to get into themselves, and the Black name was too strong. If they were caught, Black would kill them all."

I process all of his words, realizing just how connected all our families are and have been this entire time.

"So they had me steal it," I say. I can't remember ever stealing it. I don't remember breaking into the vault, but I'm sure that's where I fit into this puzzle.

"Yes. No one would suspect a young twenty-something

girl. One who could seduce and fight better than they could."

"How did I steal it?"

"You've met Zeke and me before. You flirted with us both in a bar. Zeke took an instant attraction to you; it was like nothing I'd ever seen before. He was still in love with Lucy at the time, although that relationship was ending, but you—he couldn't help but fall for you."

We didn't meet in the ocean. We met before in a bar.

"You flirted. You danced with Zeke. You stole his key to the vault."

"How could I have forgotten meeting you both?"

Langston Bishop ignores me and continues his story. "You broke into the vault and switched the boxes. You didn't know what you were doing or stealing, just that you were promised your freedom if you did this task.

"Zeke searched for you everywhere for days, hoping to find the woman who enchanted him and stole a piece of his heart."

Zeke. My heart beats for him. "How did Zeke forget me when you clearly didn't?"

"It hurt too much to remember you."

I nod, understanding. If Zeke was ever taken from me, the only way I could survive was to forget him, erase him from my memory.

"What then?"

"Then you opened the box. You realized what was inside and that you couldn't give it to them. So you hid it and killed them all. You realized it wasn't enough. Others knew of its existence. The Black family. Julian. The mystery would spread. So you started drinking, doing drugs, shock therapy —anything to make you forget so they couldn't use you to get to the box."

I blink rapidly. I forced myself to forget. Everyone Julian has done has been to get me to remember. He put Zeke into my life, hoping I would remember.

"Did you forget, or are you just a really good liar?" Langston Bishop asks.

"I can't tell a lie."

He waits, knowing that is a lie.

"At least, I couldn't tell a lie. I think all the lying and hiding of the secret maxed out my abilities. My brain couldn't process anymore lies. But lately, I've been able to lie more and more. Whatever you did to me, it started unleashing memories and allowed me space to lie again."

Langston Bishop nods.

"I think your voice in my head has actually been my father. All the words I thought you were saying were words he's said to me when he was alive."

"How do you fit into all of this? How do you know so much?"

"I needed to leave, get away for a while, my own pain was too much."

"Because of Liesel?"

Langston Bishop doesn't answer me.

"I experimented much like you did with forgetting. I needed to forget the pain. I did all sorts of horrible things—trauma can make you forget."

"Just like the trauma of killing my own parents helped me forget."

He nods.

"We're monsters."

"Yes, we are."

We both sip our tea silently before he continues.

"I ran into Julian Reed and realized he was trying to hurt my family and friends. So I stepped in, wanting to prevent

Julian from hurting them. I pretended to be on Julian's side to protect my family.

"When your husband sold you, I realized who you were. I didn't trust you initially, but then I realized you had forgotten everything. But I knew you had to remember, so I could destroy the box along with the virus inside. It was the only way to protect my family. I didn't realize at first whose side you were on. I didn't know you had hidden it to keep it safe. So I started methods to try to regain your memories. Some were painful. Remembering can be painful."

"You were trying to save us all, Langston."

He nods slightly.

He's good. He was the ultimate protector. He was trying to protect us all. He wasn't torturing me; he was begging me to remember so we could destroy the thing that could kill us all.

"Langston," I say.

He looks up at me. "Just Langston?"

I nod. He's Langston. He's good. Not evil. Bishop doesn't exist. He's just a man he was playing as he tried to save us.

"Thank you," I say.

"Don't thank me. I don't have the power to save anyone. And getting your memory back is going to hurt like hell. Only you can decide if you want to do that."

"Still, you've done a lot to help us while taking all the blame for being a monster."

Langston smirks. "Don't think I'm not still a monster. Trust me, I am. A bigger monster than all of you. I won't be accepted back into the Black family with open arms when this is all over."

"But you are on my side, Langston. You're my teammate."

"Zeke is your teammate. I'm just the man who will do what it takes to help you remember. The man you will hate for hurting you."

13

ZEKE

I LIE DOWN in the bed while I wait for Siren to come back. I consider making my presence known and kicking Langston's ass after learning that Langston has been protecting us this entire time.

But I don't trust anyone but Siren right now. I don't know if she believes everything Langston said or not, but I do know that I only trust her.

The bedroom door opens quietly and then closes.

I jump up when I see her. She's in as much shock as I am.

I don't know what to say. I can hardly think of a plan. And I'm about to spill more bad news on her. All I can do is hold her in my arms, so that's what I do.

I pull Siren tight to me, wishing my arms alone could be enough to protect her.

Time passes, probably only a few minutes, but minutes feel like hours when you're living with so much uncertainty.

"Did you hear everything Langston said?"

I nod. "Most."

I don't miss that she now calls him Langston instead of

Langston Bishop. She's decided who he is—just Langston—the good man who was once my friend. He's still my friend, just an asshole for trying to save us all instead of letting us know the truth and working with us.

If we have all learned one thing, it's when this is over, we need to learn to work together better.

Gently, I lead her to the edge of the bed so we can sit down and discuss everything that happened.

"I heard that you alone know where the box is. That it's in your memories. That's what Langston was trying to do, help you remember."

She nods.

"Did you hear the part where we met before?"

"Yes, I don't know how I could have forgotten you. Even if we only met for a second, I can't imagine ever forgetting." I take her hand and kiss it. "But I can understand the pain I must have felt at only knowing you for a moment and then losing you."

She bites her lip and tucks her hair behind her ear.

"What are you thinking?"

"Do you think everything Langston said is true?" she asks.

"Most likely. Kai called. She went back to get the box she hid. She opened it with plans to destroy it, but it was empty. Wherever it is, it's gone."

"So that means it's up to me to remember." She stands suddenly and paces as she bites her nails.

I stand to stop her from pacing, blocking her path, but she turns to pace in a smaller circle, so I grab her.

"It's going to be okay. We will make a plan. And now that you know what the dreams are about, you don't have to be afraid anymore. You can relax and let the memories come. You'll remember. And then we will destroy it."

Siren takes a deep breath, washing away some of the pain. I can't help but wonder if she's hiding something that I'm not putting together.

"I promise you, everything is going to be okay."

She puts my hand over her heart. "Tell that to my anxious heart."

Fuck, her heart is beating so fast.

There is so much more to be said. The worst hasn't even been spoken yet, but I can't stand to see her anxious.

"Undress and get in the bed," I say, deciding we need another calming round of sex to get her to relax.

"No."

"No?"

"I don't need a massage. I don't need slow and loving. I need hard and fast. I need passion and emotion. I need you to make me forget. I need you to remind me of how much my husband enjoys fucking me."

I spin her around until her ass is against my front, so she can feel my erection growing in my pants against her back. I tilt her head up and kiss her harshly, my tongue pushing past her lips, tasting every sweet drop of her.

"You want the beast inside?" I ask.

"Yes, I want my beast-man."

I give her a wicked grin. "You're going to regret saying that when you are so sore you can't walk straight for a week."

She bats her long eyelashes at me. "It will be worth it."

I tug on her hair and nip at her neck, and she moans so loudly that I'm afraid I hurt her. But I know she's just loud because she's anxious and needs to put everything into this. She needs a distraction to relax. The room is soundproof, but I've barely touched her, and she's already moaning at the top of her lungs. I've got to keep her quiet.

"Siren, baby, you are going to have to be quieter. The room is soundproof, but I'm not sure the walls can withstand your beautiful cries."

"I can't be quiet," she moans louder as I kiss her neck again.

She may want me to let my inner demon out on her, but we will definitely be caught if I do.

So instead, I decide on a different move.

I kiss her mouth, blocking some of her moans with my own mouth as I walk her into the bathroom. I flick on the shower behind her, and then I push us under the spray. The cold water chills us both, causing us to gasp before the water turns warmer.

The reaction Siren gives me is what I was hoping for. She's focused entirely on the water and me, but not as loudly as she was before.

I peel her shirt off and kiss every spot of flesh I can find on her body before caressing her breasts and pinching her nipples harshly.

She yelps at the sharp pinch of her nipple.

"Shh," I say as my hand slides down her smooth stomach and into her shorts.

"I can't. Everything feels heightened right now."

I slip my finger inside her and find her as wet inside as out.

I bite down on her shoulder to keep from screaming out myself at how perfect she is.

"I need you, Zeke. I need you, now."

"Yes."

I undo my pants and push hers down as I slide my cock between her legs, teasing her clit with my tip.

"Zeke," she cries, moaning, and I'm not even inside her yet.

I push inside her and listen to the heavenly sound leaving her throat as I pleasure her in a way only I can.

I thrust inside, and our combined ecstasy is loud enough to wake someone up a mile away. I must have left a window or the door open, because the door to the bedroom swings opens, and I hear Langston run inside.

"Siren! Are you okay? I heard screaming," he yells as he enters her bedroom, but doesn't find her.

I whisper in Siren's ear. "Tell him you are okay."

I stroke her back, but don't move my cock. She needs to tell him that she's okay to make him go away.

"Yes!" she cries, but it sounds too euphoric, there is no way he's buying that. "I'm fine!"

"You sure? Are you sick?"

"No!"

"You're scaring me. What's happening?" I hear him try the door. Even though there is no key to the bathroom, it wouldn't take much to break the lock open.

Although, it wouldn't be the worst thing for him to find me here, but until we've discussed a plan, I'd rather him not.

"Just go with it," I whisper into Siren's ear before I thrust hard into her, making her cry out.

"I'm making myself come! Go away!" She cries out as I thrust harder and harder.

She grips the side of the shower as I pump into her over and over, harder and harder with each stroke.

I hear Langston eventually retreat. I'm not sure if he believed her or not, but he's gone, and I can fuck her in peace.

So that's what I do. I drive in and out of her, watching her come more and more undone until she's screaming my name so loudly I'm afraid Langston is going to come back in here to check on her.

I finish right after her.

We don't speak as we dry off and get dressed, but I can tell she's more relaxed than she was before.

I go and double lock the bedroom door so Langston can't get in while we sleep. Then I lie down in bed with Siren, unable to keep holding my words back. I have to tell her everything.

14

SIREN

I SNUGGLE into the bed with Zeke, trying to enjoy the last few moments of lingering sex bliss. I try to mark everything in my memory, now that I know how easily my memories can be taken from me.

I remember the feel of the water raining down on my face. The feel of Zeke at my back. His hands on my body. His cock slipping in and out of me. The gruff sounds he made. The screams I made.

I memorize it all, solidifying myself for what's to come. Zeke's energy has changed to anxiety, signaling challenges we're about to face.

"Now Langston can't get in again," Zeke says.

I blush, thinking about Langston walking in on us, the sounds I was making, and what I said I was doing...

"Langston knows you are here," I say.

Zeke shrugs. "Maybe, maybe not. Does it matter anymore?"

"No, it doesn't. He told me the truth. Now we just have to decide what to do with the truth."

Zeke pulls me to him as he strokes my hair, and we lay

on our sides, staring at each other. "I have another truth to tell first."

I nod, knowing this was coming.

"Julian Reed isn't dead."

My heart shutters, but it doesn't come as a surprise. I knew deep down that Julian couldn't be killed easily. The only way is by Zeke's or my hands.

"I knew he wasn't dead."

"I'm sorry. I should have stayed. I should have killed him myself. I should have—"

I put my fingers to his lips. "No, you have nothing to apologize for. I needed you here with me."

I remove my fingers. "I wish I could have killed him and been here with you. I feel like I'm failing you."

"You aren't. You're loving me. You're protecting me. It's enough."

Zeke kisses the back of my hand. "But I can't stay and protect you here forever. I have to go back—"

"I know." I don't want Zeke to risk his life. I won't survive if something happens to him.

"We will be in Spain tomorrow. We need to make a plan," Zeke says.

I nod. "I need to stay. I need to figure out my memories with Langston."

"And I need to go kill Julian Reed."

Our fingers tangle together. Who knows how long we'll be apart this time.

It breaks my heart.

When I look into Zeke's eyes, I can see the fear in his.

"It's just temporary. A few days, maybe a week. We will be together again."

"I know, and you'll be safe. Langston will protect you; I'll make sure of that. You will take your time remembering.

There is no rush. Once Julian is dead, we will recover your memories and go destroy the box forever."

"You have to promise me that you won't put yourself at risk. That you will stop giving yourself up to save me. You will go with Kai and Enzo, and together you will all take down Julian. Promise?"

"I promise I will not put myself in excessive danger. But if it comes down to your life or mine, I will do everything I can to protect you. Don't ever make me promise differently."

I suck in a breath. I don't want to let him go. I don't want to let him risk his life without me there to fight by his side. But I can't risk my baby's life.

He tilts my head up until I can stare into his deep dark eyes. "Promise me that if you remember where the box is that you will wait until I've killed Julian and returned to go after it. We will go after it together. Your job is to remember if you can, but most importantly, your job is to stay safe. Promise me."

I kiss him. We've promised so many things. We've broken more promises than we've kept. The only promises that matter are the marriage vows we made.

"This is it. We just have to get through this final battle. This final fight, and then we will be safe," I say.

He nods. "And we will win."

But what happens after? We can't keep risking our lives like this. I can't keep risking our child's life. When this is over, our lives are going to be very different. We will have to start over, find other ways to make money, to be happy. Fighting and killing people won't work.

"So it's decided. Tomorrow I will fly to Kai and Enzo to go hunt down Julian and kill him," Zeke says.

"And I'll stay with Langston, hiding in his home, safe and doing my best to remember."

Zeke's face is filled with worry. I know how much it pains him to leave me.

"I'll text and call you as much as I can. You have the tough job. My job is just to eat and keep this baby growing," I say, rubbing my hand over my stomach, which makes him smile.

I memorize his grin. The small dimple that forms in his cheek. The light in his dark eyes.

Zeke leans down and kisses my stomach while I stroke his hair.

I try to spare him as much pain I can because he feels my pain worse than I feel it myself. I lie even though I know it's a sin, but it's a worthy sin to spare him.

The truth is, I will try to get my memories back, but it will be incredibly painful. I remember what Langston tried to do to get me to remember before. It's going to take a lot more to remember now. I have to remember to protect my family.

As long as the box is out there, my family isn't safe. The Black family is the most powerful organized crime family in the world. Hundreds of others will try and hunt the box down if they know they can use it to take down the notorious Black family.

I have to remember, no matter how painful. I have to destroy the box. But I can't let Zeke know how painful it will be, which is why Langston has to be the one to help me. I have to be strong enough to let Zeke go, and pray that he comes back.

15

ZEKE

WE'VE STOPPED MOVING, and I don't hear the purr of the engines anymore, which means we've made it to Spain.

Siren is still asleep in my arms. I want to spend every moment with her, hold onto her until the very last second, spending our last moments together kissing, hugging, and fucking.

But I have something important to do to ensure that she is safe. As much as I'd love to lay here holding her in my arms and watching her sleep, I get out of bed, shower quickly, and get dressed in my only attire of jeans and a T-shirt.

When I come back to the bedroom, Siren has stirred.

I walk over and kiss her on the head. "Shhh, sleep and take your time getting dressed. I'll be back in a few minutes."

"Where are you going?" she says with a soft smile on her face.

"I'll be back." I kiss her again. I don't have to tell her for her to know exactly what I'm doing.

I don't know how this conversation is going to go. If this

conversation doesn't go well, I may need to put Siren on a flight by herself to the farthest ends of the earth after I kill Langston.

For now, I don't want to talk about it. I just want to go deal with it and get back to our last few moments together as quickly as possible.

I head upstairs after quickly looking at the security feed to see where Langston is.

He's making breakfast in the kitchen.

I walk into the doorway of the kitchen, and Langston immediately senses me.

"Are we going to finally talk, or are you going to continue sneaking around and monitoring me on the security cameras?" Langston says, not turning around.

"When did you figure it out?"

"I suspected it when I set up the security system, but couldn't find any evidence of tampering. But after last night's show...there was no way the sounds she was making came from a vibrator."

I chuckle but try to keep it quick. We aren't back on good footing at the moment.

Langston turns around and stares at me wordlessly. He's wearing a dark grey T-shirt and jeans just like me. He looks like the same Langston I've known since I was a kid, but so much has changed. We are both different men.

"So you're married now. I never thought I'd see the day. I thought we'd both be bachelors forever," Langston finally says.

I walk forward silently.

Langston stiffens. He knows what's coming. And he deserves worse.

I punch him hard in the jaw. His head snaps—blood spills from his broken nose when he turns back to face me.

"That was for hurting my wife," I say.

He stares at me with his arms at his side. He won't fight me. He knows he deserves it, and he's preparing for another hit.

"And this is for protecting her." I grab his shoulder and pull him into a hug.

He relaxes a second and then hugs me back.

Finally, we step back, staring at each other. "Are you going to tell me why you lied to us? Why you pretended to be Bishop?"

"Partly to protect you all," Langston answers.

"And the other part?"

"My own personal shit you don't need to be concerned with."

I frown.

"I'm trying to trust you, Langston, but when you say shit like that, you don't make it easy."

"I'm not trying to make it easy. I'm just doing what I have to."

Langston's nose is still bleeding. I walk over to the sink and wet a hand-towel before tossing it to him. "Here."

He snatches it and wipes the blood from his nose. "Thanks."

"I'm going to assume the personal stuff has to do with your own woman problems?" Liesel, to be exact, if I had to guess.

"I'm not going to tell you. So if that's why you are here, you can drop it. I'm not ready to share anything except what you need to know."

I walk over to the bar and pour us both a scotch.

Langston raises his eyebrows as I hand him the drink. "I'm guessing this isn't to toast your impending fatherhood?

Although, congrats, by the way. I always thought you'd make a good father."

"No, we have other things to discuss. Come on," I sigh as we walk to a table on the top deck. We sit and look out at the city beyond the pier where we are parked.

We both sip our scotch, even though it's early in the morning. We need the drink to get through this conversation.

"Julian Reed has to be killed," I say.

Langston nods. "I agree, but you can't just kill him. You have to kill the man financing him."

"Which is who?'

Langston sips his drink. "I don't know. I tried investigating, but I never figured it out."

"We need a plan to make Julian think I'm on his side," I say.

"I thought that was what you were doing when you went with him in the helicopter."

"Yea, I was until I realized that you go by the name Bishop." I give him a dirty look.

He sighs. "Don't blame this on me."

"You hurt Siren. I blame you. You could have told me the truth when you bought her."

"I didn't realize she was yours. I recognized who she was. I knew she was the girl who flirted with you and that you fell for in the bar that night all those years ago, but I didn't realize she was yours until you bought her back from me."

"Speaking of that, you owe me the money I paid you to get her back. Don't think I forgot."

Langston chuckles. "That was fun. But it showed me just how much you love her. How far you're willing to go for her."

"Well, it wasn't fun when I didn't have the money for protecting my friends. And why did you need to test my love for her?"

"So I knew how to handle her to get her memories back."

"Now that you know, hands off her."

Langston puts his hands up mockingly. "Have I touched her since you've been monitoring me?"

"No, but it doesn't mean I trust you around her. It doesn't mean I even trust you completely yet." Although, I need to trust him in order to leave Siren with him. We all know I need to be the one to go and kill Julian, but I'll only do that if I believe in my heart that Siren and our baby will be safe.

Langston drinks his scotch wearily, leaning back in his chair as the sun rises higher behind him. We don't have much time until Siren decides to join us.

"What do you need from me to trust me again?" Langston asks.

"Show me how far you are willing to go to protect her."

Langston finishes his drink, already preparing to do whatever I ask him to do. He's one of my best friends. I don't want to see him in pain. I just want to test his loyalty. I want to see how far he's willing to go to protect Siren.

I pull a knife from my pocket and hand it to him. He takes it carefully, knowing I'm going to ask him to use it against himself.

"Cut off your finger so I know you'd be willing to lose a limb for her. That is how far I need you to go if you love her."

He sucks in a breath as he processes what I'm saying. He holds the silver knife in his hand expertly, like he could hit a man in the heart with it. He could.

But that's not what I'm asking him to do. I'm asking him to cut off a finger. Remove part of himself that he can never get back.

I don't know exactly what Langston did to try to get her memories back, but no more. The pain and torture stops now. Only slow, gentle methods from here forward. This is payback for what he did, and proof that he will do what it takes to protect her.

"Which finger?" Langston says, casually flicking the knife around in his hand.

I give him a stern look. "Your choice."

He glides the knife over each finger of his left hand, considering. I assume he'll choose his pinky, but instead, he lets the knife stop on his pointer finger.

He takes a deep breath. We have both been through plenty of pain and torture before, but none that was self-inflicted. We've hurt each other fighting and training, and been hurt countless times by our enemies, but that is as far as it has gone.

It's different inflicting physical pain on yourself rather than it being inflicted upon you. When you are tortured, you fight back. You have adrenaline pumping to keep the pain from becoming too much.

That's not true right now.

"I regret ever hurting Siren. I regret pushing her as far as I did, but Siren is a part of our family now. You love her. I will protect Siren with my life. I will do whatever it takes to keep her safe and alive. I will protect your unborn baby with my life." Langston lifts the knife above his index finger and is about to slam down. He looks me straight in the eye. "I promise to protect Siren no matter what it costs me. No matter how much I lose, I'll ensure that she lives. I vow."

And then he's slamming his arm down, intent on slicing

off his finger in one quick movement. My hand catches his wrist just as the knife hits the flesh on top of his finger.

Langston exhales harshly, surprised by my sudden movement to save his finger. The knife draws some blood, but his finger is still intact.

Langston slowly looks at me, his blue eyes dilating in surprise. "Why did you stop me?"

"I don't need to maim you for no reason. I just needed to know you were willing to do it. You'll be able to protect Siren better with all ten fingers."

Langston's shoulders relax. He gives me a curt nod in understanding.

"But if you let anyone hurt Siren, yourself included, I'll do the same thing to the woman you love." My words are harsh and cruel. And exactly how I feel.

He can deny that he loves a woman all he wants, but if he doesn't love Liesel, he definitely cares deeply for her. He wouldn't want me to lay a finger on her.

"Did I pass? Do you trust me?" Langston asks.

"Yes, I trust you. Don't make me regret it."

Langston stands and fetches the bottle of scotch, before refilling our glasses. His hand shakes as he pours, his nerves still a bit shot. He could have been faking his attempt, but based on how he's acting, it seems like he truly believed he was going to cut off his finger.

"So, what's your plan? Find Julian's financier and kill them both?"

I think for a minute. "Are you still in contact with Julian?"

"Yes," Langston says, drinking all of his scotch before he pours another glass. His hand shakes less this time.

"Does he still think you are working together toward the same goal?"

"Yes, I believe so."

"Good."

"What are you two planning without me?" Siren asks, smiling in the doorway. When I look at her, I'm glad that I didn't make Langston cut off his finger. She would be disappointed in me.

I hold out my hand, and she takes a seat on my lap. I hold her tightly, looking across the table to Langston. I'm putting everything I love in his hands.

Don't fail me, asshole.

16

SIREN

WE HAVE A PLAN, and as usual, I hate it.

One of us has to sacrifice too much to save the rest of us, but I can't think of a better option.

We are doing this as safely as possible. Kai and Enzo will be there to protect Zeke, but Zeke is still going willingly back into the lion's den. And as much as I want to be his shield, I can't.

Instead, I sit on his lap while Langston pulls his phone out to arrange everything. I'm thankful that the two of them are getting along and trusting each other again. I don't know what Langston had to do to gain Zeke's trust again, but he did. Otherwise, Zeke wouldn't be leaving me here with Langston.

Langston puts the phone to his ear, while Zeke and I sit silently by.

"Hello," Langston says.

A pause.

"I have a trade I'd like to make," Langston says.

We wait patiently for Julian to talk.

"I want in, fifty-fifty, on the box when we find it. In exchange, I'll give you Zeke."

Another pause. Langston looks up at both of us, waiting for us to stop him.

"Deal," he says and then ends the call.

"Where is the trade happening?"

"He said to meet him in Belize. I'll send my men in my place to travel with you. He knows my task is to make Siren remember, so she's safe with me. He won't interfere with trying to learn her memories."

Zeke kisses my hair.

"Good," Zeke says.

"I'll help you understand his security system and give you ideas on how to infiltrate the system before you leave," Langston says.

Zeke nods.

I stand up, and then Zeke stands. "Go get ready. I'll be right down," I instruct.

Zeke kisses me again, and then he walks downstairs.

I look at Langston. "What did he make you do to earn his trust?"

"Nothing."

I shake my head. "Liar. I know Zeke better than you do."

"Truly. In the end, he didn't make me go through with it."

"Good."

Langston stands and stares at me, looking through to my soul. "You haven't told him what you plan to do to get your memories back, have you?"

"No, I haven't."

"Why not?"

"Because if I did, he wouldn't go."

Langston frowns.

"Are you going to tell him?" I ask.

Langston looks past me. "No, I won't tell him. He feels other's pain worse than any of us. He physically can't stand to see you hurt, and I don't like hurting him."

I nod, and then I head downstairs to find Zeke preparing to leave. He's gathered all his weapons and hidden them as best as he can beneath his clothes.

"I'm not sure I'm ready for this," I say honestly. I don't want him to leave. I'm too afraid he won't come back.

Zeke holds out his hand, and I take it.

"Me neither." He pulls me to him for the hundredth time in the last few days. We're bound together like magnets, and it's going to hurt like hell when we are pulled apart.

"It's for the best, though. You need to go. Kill Julian and protect this family."

He rests his hand on my stomach. "And you need to protect our little one."

"I will."

"Kiss me."

Then our lips are smashed together, our tongues pushing and striking to bore deeper into each other's mouths. Maybe if we tangle ourselves together further, then we won't be able to be ripped apart.

It's a lie.

We both know it.

It's just going to make the separation harder.

But neither of us cares. We need this more than we need air.

Our hands find their way under each other's clothes. We don't have time to fuck, but that doesn't matter. We need each other too much to stop with just a simple kiss.

Our time is running out. These are our last moments

together. Zeke may never come back. We may both fail in our missions.

That only makes my heart beat faster, my pulse race, and my breath catch in my throat as I kiss him. I'm sure I'm a flushed mess. My hair is tangled in his fist, and my clothes are out of place, but I don't care. I never want these kisses to end.

"It's time," Langston says sadly from the doorway. Even he can't stand to make this end. But Langston's men are here to pretend to take Zeke as their prisoner to Julian, and if I don't let Zeke go, he'll miss his flight. And if that happens, I'll never let him go.

So I grab onto Zeke's shirt with my fists, as I peel my lips from his, still staying close. This is going to take everything in me to step away from him.

Zeke tucks a strand of hair behind my ear, knowing how hard this is for me as I still clutch onto him.

"This isn't goodbye," he breathes.

"I know." But I feel the tears and fear welling. We can't promise that this isn't goodbye. We can never make that promise.

"I'll come back. I won't miss the birth of our child."

"That's months away," I breathe. He better be back long before our child is born.

"I wish I could promise more. If all goes well, I'll be back in a few days, but if it doesn't..."

"It could take months." I kiss him firmly on the cheek. "Just come back to me."

"I promise."

Zeke looks down, where I'm gripping his shirt.

"I'm going to need your help," I whisper.

He clutches his hands over mine. "I'll always be with you, even when I'm not physically here."

"I'll hold you in my heart forever."

"Close your eyes, baby."

I don't want to. I know what's going to happen when I do.

"It's okay. Close your eyes."

I look at Zeke one last time, and then I close them.

"Imagine me in your head."

I do.

Zeke loosens my grip on his shirt, and then he kisses me, one last time.

"I love you," he whispers over my lips.

"I love you, too."

And then he's gone. I keep my eyes closed for as long as I can. I pretend he's still here with me, that he isn't risking his life to save our family.

Finally, I open my eyes. And as I guessed, Zeke is gone.

Langston is standing in the doorway, giving me my space. But when he sees how broken I am, he rushes over and pulls me into his arms. It's comforting, but nothing like being held by Zeke.

"You're going to get through this—you're strong." He doesn't say Zeke is going to survive, or that he's going to come back, but that I'm going to get through this. I'm strong.

His words are the truth, but it still hurts. It hurts that he can't promise me Zeke is going to be okay.

"Zeke is the strongest man I know. If anyone can survive this, he can."

I look up at Langston, and I see the truth of his words in his eyes. He believes them. That's enough for me.

I step back out of his arms and realize that I've been crying. I wipe my tears on the back of my hand. Crying isn't going to help anything. I need to be strong. I need to get to the task at hand. Zeke isn't the only one with a mission to save this family.

I need to remember where I hid the box. I need to find it and destroy it. That way, there is no reason for anyone to ever come after us again. After this is over, we will move the country and learn to raise sheep or something. We will leave this world. But first, we have to find a way to win.

I look at Langston. "How do we do this?"

He looks at me cautiously, afraid to rush me. Maybe today should just be about resting and trying to not worry, but I can't wait. I need something to do, and the sooner we figure out my memories, the sooner this can end. If I'm safe, Langston wouldn't have to watch over me. He could go help Zeke kill Julian and his men.

"Trauma can take away the memories, but it can also trigger them," Langston finally says with a serious tone.

I straighten my shoulders, standing as tall as I can. I'm not going to be defeated. I'm going to fight. I'm going to ensure my husband returns and has a family to return to.

"Then, trauma is where we will start."

17

ZEKE

I STEP out of the doorway of Siren's bedroom, and immediately the tears start.

I asked Langston to cut off his finger to show how much he would protect Siren. Walking away from her feels worse than that. It feels like I've lost an entire limb.

I know in my gut that it's the right thing to do. I know I need to leave her to protect her, but each step I take away from her still kills me.

My only comfort is that I finally believe that Langston will protect her with his life. It's not just because of all the things I've watched him do these last few days, nor because he was willing to cut off a finger for her. But because of the water tearing up in his eyes, watching me and Siren say goodbye.

Langston knows how important Siren is to me. He finally gets it. He witnessed it. I have no doubt that he will do anything to protect her.

Two men are waiting on the pier.

"You must be Zeke," the man says, extending his hand to me.

I shake it. "Yes."

"I'm Donovan. And this is Pedro."

I shake the other man's hand.

"We better get going, we have a flight to catch to Belize."

I nod and follow the men to the waiting blacked-out SUV. On the ride to the airport, we discuss strategy for how we should all behave when we meet with Julian, which keeps my brain occupied. But on the flight over, there is nothing to do but think of Siren and the life we will eventually have.

That is until the end of the flight. Donovan comes back to my seat on the private jet we chartered.

"Ready for this?"

I nod and grip the armrests to keep from reacting.

He punches me, twice in the face. Once in the stomach.

"Thanks, Donovan," I say.

He nods and then takes his seat again.

I add a couple of small rips to my shirt. The masquerade is complete. I looked like I've been through a fight, and they captured me.

Finally, we land, and I have something to focus on again other than my sorrow.

Pedro slaps some handcuffs onto my wrists that I'm more than capable of getting out of. Then he leads me to a waiting SUV to drive us the short ten-minute drive to where Julian is.

Once Pedro stops the car, Donovan takes his gun and points it at me.

"You ready?" he asks.

"Yes."

Pedro steps out of the driver's seat, drawing his gun as he opens my door and then pulls me out by the arm. Donovan steps out behind me and grabs my other arm.

They both keep their guns trained on me as we walk into the soccer field and wait for Julian to show up.

A moment later, another blacked-out car pulls up. To my surprise, Julian climbs out of the driver's seat. I don't see anyone with him.

He pulls off his sunglasses as he walks over to us.

"Here's the down payment you can give to your boss, good faith money that we will split the profits we make from the sales of the vials fifty-fifty," Julian says before tossing the bag at our feet.

Donovan picks it up and unzips it. He flicks through the money quickly, all for show.

Then he pushes me forward. "He's yours to deal with now."

Donovan and Pedro head back to the car, and I hear the spit of the gravel as they drive off. Julian and I are left to stare at each other.

We both know I could run and break free easily, so I expect Julian to draw his gun to try and control me. Then again, that's not really his style.

Instead, Julian walks to me and grabs the handcuffs around my wrists. He pops them open with his hands.

I frown, not understanding what he is doing.

"You saw Siren was with Bishop?" Julian asks me.

"Yes."

He grins. "Well, now we have our answer. Bishop is on my side, not yours."

I growl. "Tell me why I'm here, or I'm leaving. We both know those handcuffs were the only way you were going to defeat me. And now that you released me, you have no chance."

Julian laughs. "Now that you know that Bishop has Siren, I don't need handcuffs to control you. You tried going after her, but from the looks of you, you clearly lost. Bishop still has Siren. The only way you are getting her back alive is if you help me. If you run or kill me, Bishop has been ordered to kill Siren."

I shove Julian hard against his car door.

"You bastard. Don't ever threaten my wife's life."

"Help me get the box. I know you know where it is. Lucy gave it to you to hide. Tell me where it is. Help me get it back, and I won't kill Siren."

I release him.

"If Bishop so much as lays a finger on her, I'll make you wish you were dead."

"If he so much as lays a finger on her without my permission, I'll be the one making him wish he were dead." Julian turns and opens the driver's door. He doesn't pat me down. He doesn't check to see what weapons I have on me. He just climbs inside the car, knowing I will join him.

And I do. I round the car and climb into the seat next to him.

"Where to?" Julian asks, testing me.

I frown, even though inside I'm smiling. This is exactly what I wanted. I know precisely where we are going—Kai and Enzo and their team are waiting to ambush us. They will torture Julian for information about his financier, while I'll break into his phone and find out that way. We have it all planned out. It will work.

"Alaska," I say.

"Clean yourself up." Julian tosses me a towel and first aid kit. And then he starts driving.

18

SIREN

LANGSTON DRIVES me through the countryside toward his house in his convertible, with me in the passenger seat. We're headed to the same house where he held me after being captured.

Langston looks over at me. Even with his sunglasses on, I can tell by the set of his jaw and intensity flowing off him that he's nervous.

"Just tell me, Langston. After everything we've been through, I don't think anything you need to say should make you nervous."

He pauses then says, "I should warn you."

"About what?"

"You might be triggered when you arrive at the house. Last time you stayed with me, I did everything I could to make it the worst experience possible without actually hurting you in any long-lasting way. I didn't beat you. I didn't rape you. But it will still jog haunting memories most likely."

I sip on my Sprite as I gaze at the countryside, taking in what he said.

"Why do you think, when Julian raped me, it didn't trigger my memories? I had nightmares, but I still didn't remember the thing I'm desperate to remember."

"I'm nervous about that too. It should have."

"What is your theory on why it didn't?"

"It wasn't traumatic enough. As horrible as it was, it still wasn't on the same plane as you killing your own parents, as you burying a secret so deep in your brain and locking it away. It's going to take something big to unlock it."

Langston grabs my shoulder and squeezes it. "I'll be by your side the whole way. And if you would rather wait for Zeke to get back to be here with you, then we can."

I shake my head. "No. If I have to relive any trauma, it will be too hard for Zeke to bare."

"Probably," Langston agrees.

"What trauma did you live through that you were hoping to forget?" I ask, hoping that we have been friends long enough that he will tell me.

He never gives me an answer. Instead, he nods forward.

I turn and get my first glance at the place I once thought was a place of torture, but now realize was the first place for my healing.

I wait for the daydreams to haunt me, but they don't come, which almost makes it worse.

We both step out of the car, and Langston opens the door, drawing his gun.

"It's just a precaution. The security system is still up and running, but I want to be extra careful."

I nod and follow Langston in, using him like a bodyguard. He leads me to the security room, where he double checks the system and then tells me it's safe.

Only then do I explore the house a moment on my own, before Langston shows me to my bedroom next to his.

I sit on the edge of the bed. Even though today has been long, and I've had to deal with a lot, sleep won't be coming for a long time, so I might as well get to work.

"What have you tried before to get me to remember? My memory of my time here is wrong," I say.

"We don't have to start today. There is a tub in the bathroom. Why don't you take a long bath, read a book, and relax tonight?"

"No, I don't want to rest. I want to do something, try something."

If I were speaking to Zeke, he would be fighting back and ordering me around. Langston is different, though. He doesn't bark orders. But then he understands what I've been through. He knows the pain I've faced. And he, like me, wants to do something to fix this as soon as possible.

Langston sits on the edge of the bed next to me.

"I tried withholding food, putting you in a cell where you thought others were being tortured next to you, shock therapy, and drugs. I tried making you hate me, making myself into a monster that you could fight, but all it gave us were flickers of your memories. None of them were even related to the one memory we are trying to remember."

"I wish I could just make myself remember. Zeke seems to think if I give it enough time, I'll remember."

"I wish I had an easier way to help you. I've talked to all the experts, done all the research myself. The best way to remember is through a traumatic experience, something that triggers your memory.

"Although, I don't want to try any of the methods I tried before. It was one thing when you were healthy to push the limits of bringing you into a traumatic experience. It's another thing now that you are pregnant."

"So, what do you suggest we try first?"

"First, we should try the gentlest method we can."

"Which is?"

"Hypnosis. We'd bring you back to the night you met Zeke and I. Your mind may allow you to remember that happy moment, then maybe you'll remember the rest."

I nod several times. "I think that's a good idea. If for no other reason than I would love to remember the first time I laid eyes on Zeke. I would love to know if it was love at first sight or not."

"Well, it was on one side." Langston winks at me. Then he stands and holds out his hand to help me up.

I take his hand, and he helps me stand.

"Find a spot in the house where you feel calm and relaxed. I'll get my phone and play some music that will help with the hypnosis."

"Thank you, Langston."

"Don't thank me. I have no idea if this will work."

I shake my head. "Thank you for ensuring my safety." I put my hand on my stomach. "Our safety."

"Come on," he says, but I see a hint of pink cross his cheeks.

I follow him out of my bedroom, and we walk through the house to a library with gorgeous floor-to-ceiling windows.

"Will this work?" He asks me.

I nod, feeling very safe in this relaxing room.

Langston sits in the middle of the floor, so I mirror him by sitting across from him.

"Close your eyes and clear your mind," Langston says.

I do as he starts playing soft music on his phone.

I try to calm myself as I listen to the soothing music.

"Take slow, deep breaths," Langston says.

I try to slow my breathing.

"In."

I do through my nose.

"And out."

I exhale through my mouth.

His voice is calming, similar to Zeke's.

"You are safe," Langston says.

I am safe.

"Relax into your breath."

I do.

"Now think back to the first time you met Zeke. What was he doing?"

I take a deep breath and don't let the memory of finding Zeke in the ocean fill my brain. Instead, I leave my mind blank, trying to let the images come to me.

I KNOW who my targets are. Two men, boys really, similar in age to me. They work for the younger Black. They know how to access the vault. They all have access. They all have keycards and fingerprint access. The fingerprint is easy. Just get one of the many drinks they are holding and slip it into my purse. But the keycard will take more finagling.

When I step foot inside the bar where the two boys are drinking, I assume the bar will be crowded, and I won't be able to spot them easily. To my surprise, it's very easy, even though the bar is crowded, because there are only two men in the entire bar.

I thought I would have to work to figure out who they were. All I had to go by are their names—Langston and Zeke—and that they frequent this bar. I wasn't expecting that my main competition would be twenty other females all vying for their attention.

It's like they are royalty the way the women are treating them.

They are seated in a corner booth of the bar with four women around them. The rest of the women flirt or dance from afar, hoping to be summoned.

I roll my eyes as I walk to the bar and try to form a plan. I can't see the two men through the crowds of women very clearly, so I won't be able to study them from afar. I need a plan to get close.

"What can I get you?" a male bartender asks me.

"The most expensive scotch you have," I answer.

"Are you buying the guys a drink?"

"No, it's for myself."

The bartender nods at me with an impressed look.

"Can I get a credit card to open a tab for you?"

I smirk. "Who says I'll be the one buying?"

He shakes his head. "Good luck to you."

I cross my legs and watch his eyes drop to my exposed thighs. I know how to seduce like it's my job, which it is quickly becoming. I seduce men to get what I want. Or, more often, what my parents want.

"I don't need luck," I say when his eyes finally reach my face again after raking over every inch of my body. I may be wearing a dress like every other woman here, but no other woman knows how to use her curves like I do.

The bartender gapes. "You're right; you don't need luck. I'll put it on their tab."

I smile and wait for my drink before I make my move. The bartender ignores everyone else waiting and pours my drink first.

"Thanks," I say, lifting the glass as I make my way around the crowded bar. There are many seats left, which will make my ploy work even better.

There is one empty seat left at the guys' booth; they just don't realize it's empty.

I walk over like a whirlwind and drop onto one of the boys' lap.

"Excuse me? What do you think you are doing?" he asks.

"Sitting, there are no chairs open. This was the only spot I could find."

I turn my head to get a good look at the kid whose lap I'm sitting on, and my jaw drops.

This boy is all man. I was expecting a kid; instead, I got a beast. He has long dark hair, a scruffy face, dreamy eyes, and muscles for days. If he wasn't my target, I'd be head over heels in love with him right now. I can feel how fast my heart is beating, and it takes me a minute to adjust. All I know is I'm going to love using this man tonight.

"Siren? Siren, are you okay?" Langston's voice says.

I blink rapidly, looking at Langston. "I remember."

"You remember where you hid the box?"

"No, I remember meeting you and Zeke the first time." I gasp as I stand up abruptly from the ground. My head is light, and I'm dizzy as I try to process everything.

Langston grabs my elbow, keeping me steady and on my feet.

"Thanks," I mumble.

"Sit down and let me make you some tea, then you can tell me what happened."

I let Langston lead me to a large sofa, and I sit. Langston studies me closely for a second before leaving me alone.

I've met Zeke and Langston before. I can't believe it. I can't believe I have memories that I can't remember.

"Here, drink this." Langston hands me a cup of tea. I take it and sip it all down quickly, even though it's hot and burns my throat.

Langston sits next to me, takes my cup from me, pours more hot water in, and returns it to me, saying, "Slowly this time."

His eyes give me a warning to drink slowly, so I take a sip.

"What did you remember?"

"I remember coming to the bar. I remember sitting on Zeke's lap." I blush and look at Langston. "I remember falling for Zeke instantly."

Langston smiles back at me and leans back, drinking his own tea.

I raise an eyebrow. "You know drinking tea isn't the manliest thing you could be doing. You could drink alcohol if you want, I don't mind."

"I don't want to drink alcohol, and I'm perfectly comfortable in my own manhood."

I smile at that.

"I'm glad you remember meeting Zeke. I've been so annoyed that neither of you could remember while I'm stuck remembering witnessing you two exchanging sappy words and constantly flirting."

I tuck my hair behind my ear as I lean back on the couch with my cup of tea resting in my lap. "I can't believe how much our lives have been intertwined this whole time. I can't believe how different my life could have been if I decided to take a chance on Zeke then, instead of now."

"You can't think like that. If you and Zeke had started dating then, you would have been on the yacht when Zeke was shot. You would have thought he was dead along with us. No one would have been there to save him. You couldn't be together then because you needed to save him so you could be together now."

I look at Langston sitting next to me. I don't know how I

could have ever mistaken him for a monster, when he's clearly a kind man who truly cares about his family.

"Thanks for saying that. I needed that."

"Don't," Langston tenses.

"Don't what?"

"Don't think I'm a good man. I'm not your savior. I'm barely your friend. Don't ever mistake me for more than I am."

"Who are you, then?"

"I'll protect you, but I'll also look out for my own interests. I'll do horrible things that I'll never explain to you or anyone else. I'll protect you, but don't think that protection lasts forever like Zeke's."

I nod, but I don't believe his words. I don't think Langston could ever stop protecting me. The only thing he would ever let get in the way of protecting me would be his love for another woman in a situation worse than mine.

"I love you too, Langston." I wink at him.

He blinks rapidly like he's never heard those words spoken to him before.

I laugh. "I'm not in love with you, but I love you like a brother. And I will do everything in my power to protect you too."

He rubs the back of his neck. "How could you love me when I've been so cruel?"

"Have you been that cruel?" I throw his own words from earlier back at him as I smile behind my cup of tea.

He shakes his head, and I decide not to push the conversation further.

"So what do we do now? I remember meeting you, but I don't remember anything after that. I don't remember stealing the box. I don't remember hiding it." I don't remember killing my own parents.

"Now, we try to get some sleep. Tomorrow we will try to push you further."

I shudder, but I know he's right as I yawn.

"We should go to bed," Langston says.

I agree. However, I don't want to be alone right now. Zeke is gone. He hasn't texted or called. We don't know if he's still alive or hurt. We don't know what's happening.

So I set my cup down on the end table and then curl my legs up beneath me and lean onto Langston's chest. He stiffens at first, but slowly he puts his arms around my back, holding me against him.

"Zeke is going to kill me for this."

I laugh. "He would until I told him that you were just being a good brother and helping me keep the nightmares away."

"I can do that."

I close my eyes and try to sleep. The nightmares will stay away as long as Langston is here, but I'm afraid what I need to do to remember is let the nightmares in.

19

ZEKE

WE ARRIVE in Alaska at Kai and Enzo's house up here. I feel weird about using their house to attack Julian and commit murder when this place is such a sanctuary for them, far away from all the evil in their lives. But we know the area and the land, so we'll have an advantage here.

"Where is it?" Julian asks as he parks the SUV we rented in front of the house.

"In a security box in the basement."

Julian pulls out his gun and motions for me to do the same. "Remember what will happen if you turn on me."

"I get the box, turn it over to you, and Siren goes free. I got it. I won't betray you. I tried that, and I failed."

Julian snickers.

God, I'm going to enjoy killing Julian more than any other man I've killed. I hope Enzo and Kai don't kill him before I get a chance to hurt him.

I keep my eyes peeled for any sign of them or their men as we walk up to the front door. I haven't texted or had contact with them since Langston's men turned me over to Julian, so I don't know where they are hiding or when they plan on attacking Julian. But I'll be ready, and I can't wait to finally give the bastard what he deserves.

I pick the lock on the door and open it, sticking my gun in first before stepping inside.

Julian follows right after me, practically using me as a human shield—*coward*.

I continue through the house, but I don't see any sign of anyone. Enzo and Kai are very talented assassins, so they won't make themselves known until the last second. Still, it unsettles me to have no hints as to where they are.

"Where is the basement?" Julian asks.

I scan the room. "This way."

I start heading down the hallway, toward the basement door. I open it, and we walk downstairs carefully. I don't bother with the lights, and neither does Julian.

"There," I say, pointing to the safe sitting at the far end of the room.

"Good, now unlock it."

I snarl. Of course, he won't be doing any of the work himself.

I walk to the safe and tuck my gun away, going to work on picking the safe. I only know how to do it because the Black family deals in security systems. Otherwise, a system like this can't be opened.

I take my time, assuming now is when Enzo and Kai are going to choose to ambush Julian.

But when I hear the final click of the lock before the safe pops open, there has been no ambush.

"The safe is unlocked," I say, stepping away from it.

Julian steps forward after putting his gun away. I take mine out and scan around the darkness, trying to look for Kai and Enzo to give them the signal.

Finally, I see the whites of men's eyes staring back at me. I see guns. They aren't pointed at Julian.

Fuck.

Julian opens the safe and pulls out the box that Siren hid here after stealing it from the vault. The box once held a secret weapon; instead, the box is now empty.

Julian opens it easily. The latch is already broken open from Kai and Enzo.

Julian doesn't seem surprised to find it empty. Instead, he whistles.

The lights flick on, and two dozen men step forward with their guns aimed at me. Then I see them, Enzo and Kai, tied up with guns trained on them.

Julian tosses the box to the ground. His eyes have darkened, but otherwise, there is no sign of anger as he walks toward me.

"I thought you cared more about your wife's life than this. But I guess I was wrong; you don't care about Siren at all."

My body fills with rage. "All I care about is Siren."

"Then stop lying to me. Stop trying to trick me!"

"Stop trying to kill my family!"

Julian shakes his head before he walks over to Enzo. It's the first I've seen Enzo since I shot him. I'm glad the damage I did was minimal. My eyes skim to Kai, who doesn't seem upset with me in the least, even though deep down she'd love to have my balls for daring to hurt her husband.

I flick back to Julian, who is patting Enzo on the cheek. "Look at that—he isn't dead. Isn't that what I asked of you? For you to kill him?" Julian punches his shoulder where I shot him. Enzo doesn't flinch, restricted by the restraints around his wrists, arms, and ankles. Julian grabs his shirt and rips it open, finding no bullet wound.

Julian turns to me and hisses through clenched teeth. "Lies...all you lot can do is lie."

He walks over to me, getting in my face, even though I'm a foot taller than him.

"You do realize that I hold all the power? I have everything, and you have nothing. If you don't do exactly as I say from here on out, you'll lose everything you hold dear."

My chest rises and falls as I focus on my breathing instead of snapping his neck. It would make me feel better for a split second, before the rain of bullets his men would send down on me and my friends a second later.

"What do you want?" I ask.

Julian tsks. "No, you don't get to ask that. First, you have to be punished for what you did here today."

"Whip me, beat me, torture me. You can do whatever you want to me. It won't leave a dent on me. It will be nothing compared to what I've already experienced."

Julian pulls out his cell phone with a grin.

I stiffen but remember Langston is on my side. He won't let anything bad happen to Siren. There is nothing to fear. I just have to let Julian know how afraid I am.

Julian dials a number, then puts the phone to his ear.

"Don't," I beg.

He laughs. "You lied. You get punished."

He turns his attention back to the phone. "Bishop, I need you to do something for me."

I wait for Langston to speak back.

"I need you to punish Siren for Zeke's disloyalty. I need you to make her scream now on the phone so we can all hear."

My eyes widen, and my heart stops.

Langston won't really hurt her. Whatever screams Siren makes will be fake. *They will be an act. They won't be real.*

Julian pulls the phone from his ear and puts the phone on speakerphone. Thank God he didn't ask to video chat and show him beating Siren, that would be harder to fake. And if Julian saw Siren, he might realize that she's pregnant.

There's a scuffle.

Then I hear Langston say, "Come here, bitch."

It's an act. It's all a lie.

I look over at Enzo and Kai, who both fight against their bindings to stop Langston. They, too, know it's fake, but it's still hard to not react. It's also what they would be doing if they didn't know it was fake. I need to let myself react more to sell this.

"Julian, stop this. I'll do whatever you want. I'll help you find where the real box is. Just don't hurt Siren," I beg.

"I have Siren tied up. Should I continue, Julian?" Langston says.

Julian's grin turns up slowly, and it looks the devil himself is possessing his body.

"Yes," he says.

"No!" I scream, running to Julian.

But it's too late.

I hear a whip-like sound, followed by Siren howling. I don't know how he made the noises without striking actual flesh, which scares me.

Siren is fine. Langston promised. He promised.

Another whip, though, and the scream from Siren this time is horrific. It echoes through my ears and lands in my heart. I never want Siren to hurt. I can't stand for her to hurt. It feels worse than a thousand whips hitting my back all at once.

"Please, stop this," I beg Julian.

Julian just cocks his head and licks his lips in enjoyment. "Three more," he says into the phone.

Three more. I can't stand it, even though I know it's fake. I can't listen to her scream three more times.

"Please!" I get down on my knees in front of Julian, begging him to stop this, to end this.

I hear another strike, another scream. Her voice is high-pitched, and it sounds like she's losing her voice or crying.

She can't be, though, not my strong Siren.

Another strike. Another scream. Another piece of my fragile heart breaks, and I feel tears watering my eyes. Apparently, I don't need to act at all. As much as I thought I was certain that Langston was on our side, this is Bishop. And Bishop, I don't trust.

I close my eyes as the fifth and final strike is delivered, followed by a scream that splits my soul.

It's not real. She's not in pain. The baby isn't in danger. This isn't real.

"That's enough for now," Julian says into the phone before hanging up.

He walks over to me.

"Stand up," he commands.

I do. We always had a plan that if we failed, I would fall in line. Get him to trust me, figure out his financial backer, and then find a way to kill them all.

"Now, one of you three knows where the box is. Tell me, or we will go through that entire exercise again."

20

SIREN

I DIDN'T HAVE to fake my screams or tears. If Julian wanted Langston to hurt me, it could only mean one thing—Zeke failed. He got captured for real, and I don't know if he's going to survive.

My emotions ran high as Langston handed me the whip and told me to strike his back each time Julian asked. I didn't hit him very hard, just enough to make a horrible sound over the phone. It was enough that Langston had to bite down on a belt to keep from making a sound.

But my cries of pain were real. They weren't because of the physical pain I was in, but because of my fear of losing Zeke, of my child growing up without a father. I can't stand the thoughts.

I made the wrong decision in letting him go back to fight Julian Reed alone. I should have sent Langston with him. I should have gone with him. Or he shouldn't have gone at all.

Langston ends the call, and instead of worrying about the pain I inflicted on his back, he holds me close in a deep hug as I collapse to the floor.

"Julian has Zeke. He failed. He's going to die. I can't lose him," I sob into Langston's shoulder.

"Shhh, Zeke isn't going to die. He had a plan for this, remember? He's strong. He's not going to let anything stop him from coming back for the birth of his first child."

"That's months away."

"Yes, and I suspect he'll be back a lot sooner than that. But you have to stay strong, so Zeke can stay strong."

I nod vigorously—Langston's right. I'm being ridiculous. Zeke is obviously still alive or Julian wouldn't call. And I heard Zeke's voice in the background. Zeke is alive. He'll win this war in the end.

"Let me look at your back." I turn Langston around. "Oh my god!" I gasp. "I didn't mean to hit you so hard." Red welts pop up on his back.

Langston brushes me off. "I'm fine. You shot me, remember? That was much worse. You just got into it a little when you were feeling all the pain."

"Let me get you something to soothe your back, though." I'm off before Langston can stop me.

I run to the bathroom, catching my breath before finding some salve to rub on his back. Zeke is strong. He's going to survive. I have to remain calm for my baby.

I grab the bottle of salve and then run back to find Langston still sitting shirtless in the living room.

"This should help," I say as I squirt some into my hand and then rub it on his back. He doesn't flinch or react when I touch him.

"Is that better?" I ask.

"Yes. Thanks, Ren," Langston says.

"Ren, huh?" I sit down on the couch while Langston stands from the floor, puts on his shirt, and then sits next to me.

"I know Siren is the name Zeke calls you. It feels as much as an endearment as it does your real name. And no one seems to call you Aria. What do you prefer I call you?"

I smile. "Ren sounds perfect, Lang."

He laughs at my shortening of his name, but I notice him wince slightly when his back hits the back of the couch. I hurt him more than I intended.

"Wait here, one sec." I rush off and come back with a bottle of whiskey and a glass for him. I pour and hand him a full glass.

"Thanks," he says, staring at the glass a second before drinking it quickly. I pour another shot into the glass, and this one, he sips slower.

He looks at me, studying me closely. "Did it trigger any new memories?"

I shake my head sadly.

"What do we do now? We've tried hypnosis and meditation. They haven't worked."

He bites his lip, and I know what he's thinking but doesn't want to suggest.

"What is it?" I ask. "It can't be as bad as you think it is, just tell me."

"You killed your parents right after hiding the box, right?"

"Yes, I assume so."

"Then maybe killing someone is the answer."

I frown. "But I've killed people before. It didn't trigger anything."

"True, but you are in a very emotional state right now. Combine that with killing someone, and it just might do it."

I nod, it makes sense. "I'm not just going to go kill an innocent person in hopes that I can remember where I hid a box. Even if finding the box first might save millions."

"I'm not asking you to kill an innocent person. Your parents weren't innocent."

I take a deep breath. It's a better idea than Langston trying to torture me, but Zeke will kill me if I put myself into danger trying to remember.

"I won't let you be in any danger."

"I know," I exhale a deep breath. "So, where are we going to find a bad guy who is easy to kill and doesn't put me at too much risk?"

Langston downs his drink. "Come on, we have a bad guy to hunt down."

He holds out his hand, and I take it.

"Where are we going?"

"You still got your gun and knife on you?"

"Always."

"Good, then let's go." He drags me to his car before I have time to process what we are doing. Then we are driving down the road, destination unknown.

"What are you thinking about?" he asks.

"Zeke."

"Good, keep thinking about him."

So I do. I let the fear of losing him in, even though I know it comes with some anxiety. I let it in. I let all my emotions in. I feel all my worry as we drive.

Finally, Langston stops in an alleyway.

"Where are we?"

"A local bar."

"I don't think anyone deserves to die just because they like to drink."

"We aren't killing someone because they drink too much. We are killing a known rapist."

It's like Langston hit me with a bolt of lighting. Rage erupts in me to be near a man inside this bar who raped other women. That is not something that should ever happen.

"How do you know?"

"He paid the judge to throw out the case. I've seen the evidence; it was all over the local papers here. He's guilty. He owns this bar, and not a single woman will enter for fear of what he will do to them."

I let my anger flow through me.

"Name."

"Fred Parry."

"Do you have a picture?"

"No, you aren't going inside the bar. You'll wait here, and I'll drag him out—"

"No, I'm going. We are trying to trigger my memories. I need to be as involved as possible."

"It's not—"

"Safe? This man is a rapist, not an assassin. I have a gun and a knife. I have a badass bodyguard. I'll be fine." My eyes shoot into Langston, not giving him a choice in the matter.

He nods.

We jump out of the car and start walking toward the bar side by side. I'm focused on my mission. There is nothing that gets my adrenaline going more than killing an evil, vile monster. I'm going to enjoy this a little too much.

We walk into the bar, and as Langston said, there are no women. The scene is the exact opposite of when I found Zeke and Langston in their bar all those years ago.

"I never asked, why was there only women in the bar when I met you?"

"We were stupid playboys who didn't realize that women like you and Kai existed. Otherwise, we wouldn't have been wasting time just getting laid every night."

"Good answer." I look around as all the men's eyes stare at me with a silent hunger.

"I'm looking for a Mr. Fred Parry," I say loudly. I suspect that if I killed several men in this bar, it would all be deserved.

None of the men answer me.

I look to Langston, who they will answer to.

"Where is Fred Parry?" Langston says, his voice booming with an aura of authority.

A man points in the direction of the back.

"Carry on," I say as we walk through the bar like we own the place. Langston stops at the back door and steps through first with his gun raised.

I follow after. I would prefer to walk in first, but it's safer to enter second.

We walk through a short hallway to an open door that leads to a cramped office. Two men are smoking a cigar around a desk.

"Fred Parry?" Langston asks the man sitting behind the desk.

"Yes, who the bloody hell are you? You aren't supposed to be back here. Get out!"

Langston shakes his head and then grabs the other man by the back of the shirt. "You, get out."

"But—" the man mumbles.

"Get. Out." Langston growls to the man who finally spots the gun he's holding. The man scurries out so fast that you'd think his feet were on fire.

I step inside the office next, shutting the door behind me with a thud.

"What the hell is this?" Fred yells at us, his voice gruff from years of smoking, no doubt.

"We are here to deliver justice," I say.

Fred laughs, turning into a cough of smoke. "Justice? Like there is such a thing."

"Well, you are about to find out how justice works," I say.

I walk over to his desk, grab him by the back of his neck, and turn him in his chair to me. He tries to fight me off him, but I only hold on harder.

"Did you rape a woman in this very bar?"

He narrows his eyes. "Go to hell."

I slam his head down on the desk.

"Did you rape someone?"

His throat tightens, his face now bloodied from a most likely broken nose, but he realizes that I'm serious.

I move to slam his head down again.

"Yes!" he screams. "Yes, I raped her."

"Just her?" I ask sternly.

"No, I've raped six other women."

So much emotion pours through me. The thought that Zeke could die from a man who raped me has me on edge. Holding this rapist's neck sets me on fire.

I want to burn this whole place down. I can feel the energy in this room. He brought the women here. He raped them here, most likely on this very desk. After I kill him, I will burn this bar to the ground. I will ensure the women have their justice.

I slam his head down again, and the man screams like he's being tortured. He has no idea what torture feels like—yet.

"Please, I have money. I can pay you," the man pleads.

God, he disgusts me. Like I would want to take money from a man like him.

I look to Langston, who is leaning against the wall watching this happen.

"Leave us. I'd like to have a little chat alone with Mr. Parry here."

Langston frowns. He doesn't want to leave me alone, but I can handle this vile man. He's not dangerous, and I need to let all the feelings flow if I have a chance at getting my memories back.

"I'll be right outside," Langston says before stepping out. He'll be listening and will barge back in at any second if I need him.

I nod. He shuts the door to the office, leaving me and Mr. Parry alone.

I consider torturing the man. He deserves it, but I don't think it will help me get my memories back, and it won't heal me.

But Fred won't be walking out of this office alive.

"What do you want then?" Fred asks with a shaky voice.

I consider his question. I want his death. I want to spill his blood on the table where he tortured people. *But other than that, what do I want?*

"Why? Why did you do it?" I ask, realizing that's what I want. To know why a man rapes. *Why was I raped? Why, when Julian could have convinced any number of women to sleep with him? Why, when he could have paid for the pleasure? Why take from me? Why am I not more hurt by the pain I experienced?*

The man stares at me, blinking like I can't be serious to ask such a question. That's when I realize that there is no reason. There is just something dark inside that drives some men to do bad things.

I close my eyes and let my own rape fill my head. I let all the dark images of Julian being on top of me, hurting me, taking from me. I remember it all. Not the images of Zeke that I filled my head with to hide my pain, I let the real truth come through.

Until my hands are clammy and shaking. Until my breath has sped up. Until I'm afraid this man standing in front of me could do the same thing to me unless I stop him.

Only then do I open my eyes and pull the trigger.

The man falls dead in front of me in a single shot. I stare at his lifeless bloodied body. He got off easy.

I close my eyes and try to remember my parents, my pain then. My horror at finding out that the box I stole for them was dangerous to the world, and what their intentions were.

But all I see is Julian.

"Damn," I curse under my breath, knowing that this trauma isn't close enough. I don't know what is, but this isn't.

The door opens, and Langston looks from me to Fred then back to me with a question in his eyes.

I shake my head.

"We can try again."

"No, I need to think more about it. As much as I'd love to scour the entire city, ridding it of all the rapists and murders, I need to find something else, something that doesn't remind me of my own rape."

Langston nods. "Let's get out of here."

I follow Langston out into the hallway. I find the fire alarm and pull it, ensuring the bar empties out. Then I walk into the main bar, now empty, and pull out a bottle of rum. I drench everything in sight. Then light a match and toss it on the bar.

It immediately catches fires. The bar will burn. This

place will be lost to history. The women will get their justice.

"Come on, we should go," Langston says as sirens sound in the distance.

I follow Langston out the back, the heat of the fire warming our backsides.

I stop suddenly, an unusual cold washing over me.

"What is it?" Langston stops abruptly, holding my biceps as he stares down at me.

"I don't know. Just a coldness washed over me. A dark chill. Something's wrong."

I meet Langston's eyes, and I don't have to tell him what I think it means. *Something has happened to Zeke.*

Langston pulls out his phone, and we both look down at the missed call flashing on the screen.

It's from Julian.

Fuck.

21

ZEKE

"WHO WANTS to tell me where the real box is? Hmm?" Julian asks as he looks from me to Enzo and Kai. They're bound still, but standing on their own.

I'm the only unrestrained one, but with a dozen guns aimed at me, I'm as tied up as they are.

None of us speak. I need a plan. *If we give him a random destination and there is no box there, then what?* We are no better off than we are now. And he might kill us and go search for it himself. He doesn't realize Siren knows. He thinks we have it and hid it.

I could kill Julian now, as I still have my gun, but I'd be risking my friend's lives. No, now isn't the time. I need to give them a chance to break free first. Then, I can figure out who Julian's backer is and kill them both.

"No one wants to speak, huh? Should I get Bishop back on the phone?" Julian takes his phone out again and dials a number.

"Rot in hell," Kai yells at Julian, drawing his attention to her. He holds out the phone, and we all watch it ring as he walks toward her.

Don't pick up. Don't pick up.

I can't handle listening to Siren screaming again. I'll lose my mind.

The phone stops ringing, playing a voicemail recording.

Julian ends the call as he licks his lips, staring at Kai like he's just realized she's a woman.

"Too bad for you," Julian says to Kai.

Enzo and I lose it at the same time. Julian will not touch Kai. He will never touch another woman who doesn't willingly give herself over to him.

I charge at Julian from behind, while Enzo trips Julian up, keeping him from touching her.

I grab onto Julian, and we tumble to the ground. I punch him hard. My rage overflows in me, rage at what he wanted to do to Kai, at what he did to Siren. All other thoughts of how to keep everyone safe fly out of my mind.

I punch him viciously in the face, drawing blood from his mouth. I probably knocked a tooth loose. I punch three more times before arms go around me, pulling me up.

Guns are pointed at me, but no one shoots. They may torture us, but they won't kill us. They don't know which one of us has the information. They think we are protecting ourselves by not spreading the information through our group. They don't realize that none of us knows. The only person who knows is Siren, and her memories are locked away at the moment.

"Shoot me. Kill me. None of us will ever tell you where the box is," I taunt Julian.

He glares at me with a bruised and bloodied face. It felt good to punch him.

Julian approaches me when his phone rings again.

He stops and pulls it out of his pocket.

I try to fight to get free from the men holding me back,

but I can't. From the timid look on Julian's face, it's not Langston calling him back.

"Yes," he says sternly.

Pause.

"Not yet, sir."

Sir. This must be the man financing this whole venture.

"Yes, sir."

Julian hangs up. "Everyone out." His eyes hang on me, letting me know I'll be staying.

The guards start dragging Kai and Enzo out, which is a good thing. They will be safe away from Julian.

"Tie him up first, then leave us," Julian says to the guards holding me back.

They tie my wrists behind my back, and my ankles together, before leaving me standing in the room alone.

"Coward. You can't even fight me without me being tied up," I spout.

"I'm not going to fight you. I'm going to make you see reason."

"Yea, and what reason is that?"

"I need the box. And you need Siren to survive. We need each other."

"No, you need me. I don't need you."

"You have until Bishop calls me back to tell me where the box is, or who among you knows. If you don't, I'll have him rape Siren. If that doesn't do the trick, I'll have him kill her."

"If you do that, you'll have nothing to hold over me."

"Time is running out. I don't have any choice anymore."

"You mean, your boss has grown impatient and wants results."

He growls at me before taking his phone out. He types a quick text message to Langston and then hits send. He holds up the phone to show it to me. *Tie up Siren and then FaceTime me.*

Fuck, no. How is Langston going to be able to hide what he's doing to Siren if it's on video?

"Tell me, and this all ends. Tell me where the box is. Tell me who knows where it is hidden, and I won't give Bishop the order."

I grit my teeth. I don't know how to stop this.

"Your problem is with me, take it out on me like a man."

"No, you've been tortured and near death too many times. The only thing that even comes close to bringing you pain anymore is when I hurt Siren."

"You care about Siren too, don't let another man hurt her."

"I don't take enjoyment in having another man touch a woman who I feel is mine. But since I had her first, I think I can make an exception."

The phone rings. I stare at it—a video call from Bishop.

I squeeze my eyes closed and then open them again, hoping to God this isn't happening, that it's all a nightmare.

But when I open them again, Julian is answering the phone call.

"Hello, Bishop, so happy you could call me back."

"Since I don't exactly work for you, I don't have to be at your beck and call or tell you what I'm doing. This is a partnership."

"Yes, of course. But I think you're going to like where our partnership is headed. Is Siren tied up?"

"Yes," Langston says, moving the phone so I can see Siren tied in a similar fashion to me, except she's seated. She's wearing a loose sweatshirt that hides her belly with black leggings underneath.

A beautiful and heartbreaking sight.

"Zeke here needs a little motivation to tell us where the box is," Julian says.

The camera is still pointed at Siren. "Don't tell him anything!" she shouts at me.

"Siren! Baby!" I cry out.

"Hush," Julian orders, muting the phone so that my voice can no longer be heard. When I'm quiet, he unmutes it and speaks.

"Slap her."

Langston does. I hear the slap of her cheek. The redness is growing. It was a real slap. There was no way to hide it. No way to fake it.

"One last chance," Julian says to me.

I'm sweaty. I'm broken. I can feel every bit of her pain. I can't watch Langston try to fake his way through hurting her. He'll have no choice but to hurt her or reveal the truth. It's best if Julian still trusts Langston. And if for some reason I'm wrong, and Langston really is on Julian's side and not mine, then I need to protect Siren.

"Stop this, and I'll talk," I say.

Julian walks over to me. "Start talking."

"I need to know that everyone is safe. Release Kai and Enzo in good faith that you will release Siren and me when the time comes."

"No."

"Then I'm not giving you the information," I say, and hope to death that Julian won't push Langston any further to hurt Siren.

Julian studies me. Both of us need to win this war, not wanting to back down.

Whoever blinks first will show weakness. *How far will I push this before I crack and protect Siren at all costs? How desperate is Julian to know the information?*

"I'll leave Kai and Enzo here tied up with two guards. It will take them some time to break free, but they are more than capable of getting them untied and taking down two guards while we go get the box. That is the best I will do."

"Deal," I say, knowing that is as far as I can push him while also protecting Siren's life.

"So, where is it?"

"I don't know."

"Who knows?" Julian gets in my face.

I have to make a decision. I've tried fighting Julian apart and failed. And as much as I don't want to let Julian anywhere near Siren, I think the best decision is to be together. Together we can take him down. Langston can help. It's the only way I can think to save us all.

Julian reads it on my face. I don't even have to tell him.

"Siren knows," he says after muting the phone.

"Yes," I say. At least it keeps him from killing her if he thinks she knows where the box is. But it doesn't save her from being tortured. Although, maybe he'll torture me to get her to speak. So I add, "And her only weakness is me."

Julian grins. "I'm going to enjoy torturing you while I persuade my Aria to talk."

Good. As long as you don't touch her, do whatever you want to me.

Julian picks up the phone and unmutes it. "We are headed to you. We will be there in twenty-four hours."

"Do you know where the box is?" Langston asks back.

"No, but we will soon," Julian says and then hangs up before calling in his guards to carry me to the car still tied up. Julian thinks he needs to keep me tied up, but he doesn't. I won't fight him, bringing me back to Siren. That I will never fight.

Langston, you better be ready to take this motherfucker down. There is no way I'm going to let him touch Siren.

22

SIREN

Langston hangs up the phone.

"I'm so sorry," Langston runs over and unties my ankles and wrists while staring at my face where he slapped me.

"I had to make it look real. I'll go get some ice."

"No, I'm fine. I can handle a slap. I'm just thankful he didn't ask you to do more."

We both still, knowing how far Julian could have asked Langston to go. He could have had him whip me, or even rape me. And short of telling the truth, that Langston is on our side and not Julian's, there was nothing we could have done.

We both know it—how close we came.

"I'll do everything I can to protect you; you know that, right?" Langston says.

"Yes, I do."

"The good news is that Zeke's alive. Let's focus on that."

"Except we can't focus on that. They are coming here. We have to unlock my memories, find the box, and destroy it. Our time has run out."

Langston runs his hand through his blonde hair.

"Unlocking your memory isn't something we can rush. We've tried everything. I don't think there is anything left to try."

I tilt my head. "We haven't tried everything."

His eyes narrow as he tries to make sense of my words. "You're right; we haven't. You killed someone you loved. You did it to protect the world, but you still did it."

"I'm not going to kill anyone I love, not again."

I stand up and walk out of the room, through the door to the back deck, needing some fresh air. I know what Langston is going to suggest, and I'm not doing it.

Langston gives me a minute before he steps out onto the deck and leans against the railing next to me as we both look out at the garden below.

"We don't have a choice."

"I'm not going to kill you in hopes that I might remember."

"Then what do you suggest?"

I bite my lip as I rack my brain for any idea other than killing Langston.

"We should think about where I might have hidden it. What choices I had available to me at the time. Send someone to search in those places if we can't look ourselves."

Langston turns around and leans his elbows on the railing. "Okay, you were in your early twenties. What resources did you have? How much money did you have available to you?"

"I didn't have much money."

He nods. "That's good. Then it's probably still in Florida somewhere. Or St. Kitts, where you met Julian and your ex-husband?"

I frown.

"What?" His brows furrow.

"I didn't have money. But my best friend, Nora, had endless amounts of money."

"Okay, but would she have lent you money?"

I nod. "It gets worse."

"How could it get worse?"

"Nora has her pilot's license. She owned a private plane. She could have flown me anywhere."

Langston stares, his eyes widen.

I could have hidden it anywhere. Literally, anywhere.

"Nora," we both say at the same time.

We run back inside and grab my cell phone. I dial Nora's number.

"Pick up, pick up," I mutter. I know her and Beckett are in charge of keeping the twins safe. Calling her on a phone that might be traceable is dangerous for them, but not finding the box first is more dangerous.

"Siren, what is it? What's wrong?" Nora answers.

I exhale a breath as Langston stares me nervously.

"I need to ask you an important question."

"Okay, what is it?"

"Do you remember back when I made a trip to Miami just before my parents died?"

"Yes, I remember. You were so despondent afterward. You wouldn't talk about it. And then shortly after you got married."

She remembers. Thank goodness.

"Do you remember me asking you to fly me anywhere or borrow any money? Maybe I asked you to fly me somewhere after Miami or right after I returned to the island?"

"No, you couldn't have asked me to fly anywhere. I didn't get my pilot's license until the following spring."

Dammit.

"What about money? Do you remember me asking you to borrow any money?"

Nora sighs. "I wish you would have asked to borrow money. But you never did, you hated being a burden."

I run my hand through my hair as I sink down in the chair. I was so hopeful that Nora would be able to give us a clue, but once again, I come up empty.

"Can you remember me talking about hiding something? About a trip somewhere? A new security box I purchased? Anything like that?"

"I wish I could, but you didn't talk much during that time. You started down a bad path, and then you found Hugo. And then everything else spiraled after that."

There's a pause.

"You don't remember that time, do you?" Nora asks.

"No, that's what Langston was trying to do, spark my memories."

I'm about to hang up the phone when Nora says, "I don't know if this helps at all, but I do remember something weird that happened a year later."

I sit up, hopeful.

"I was talking about all the places I wanted to go for my birthday and trying to convince you to go with me. I mentioned that we should go to Scotland, and the look you gave me was like all the blood had been sucked out of you.

"I asked you if you had you been there before. You said no, but your reaction was wrong. You shouldn't have had that strong of a reaction. We never talked about it. But we also never traveled to Scotland."

"Scotland," I repeat.

"I don't know if it's helpful, but maybe start there. Something bad happened there."

"Thank you, Nora. I want to ask how you are doing, but I

shouldn't know anything about where you are or how you're doing. It would put you at risk. Tell Beckett that I called and to make sure your phone isn't traced."

"Ugh, I can't stand Beckett."

I frown. "I thought you had the hots for him."

"I do, but that doesn't mean he isn't the most insufferable know-it-all, who even wants to lecture me on how to take care of two little ones."

I smile. "Is your problem that he is right and does know more about babies than you?"

She sighs. "Yes, but I should be the one who knows more. I'm the woman!"

I laugh. "Beckett spent weeks taking care of them on his own before. He's been their uncle for months now. The babies are named after him. I don't think it's wrong that he knows more than you."

"He doesn't have to rub it in my face, though."

I bite my lip to keep from laughing again.

"I need to go, Nora. Stay safe. And don't forget to tell Beckett about this call."

"Yea, yea, so he can come to my rescue and save me."

"He's saving the babies, not just you."

"I guess." I can practically hear her rolling her eyes. "Stay safe. Hope to see you soon."

We end the call, and I look at Langston.

"Scotland, that's all she could give me," I say.

Langston runs off, returning a minute later with his laptop. He pulls up Scotland on a map and starts zeroing in different places.

"Anything look familiar to you or stand out?"

I stare at the map, a cold feeling washing over me. I take the computer from him and place it on my lap. I roam the cursor over the screen, hoping that something will trigger my memories.

I could have hidden it anywhere in the country —anywhere.

By the sea.

In the cities.

Buried in the sand.

Or in the mountains.

Locked in a lockbox.

Secured in a safe.

Getting a country to focus on is no more helpful than knowing that I hid it somewhere in the world. There are simply too many places to search.

I zoom in and put it on satellite view so that I can see the buildings and streets, hoping something will help me to remember. The familiar look of a building. The name of the street. Anything.

"Siren?" Langston eventually says, taking the laptop from me and closing it.

I blink rapidly and then stare at him.

"You've been looking at the screen for over an hour. If you were going to remember something, I think you would have remembered by now."

"I'm sorry. I'm just terrified that I won't remember, but that Julian will. If he figures out where it is before us, then we are all doomed."

"Don't put this all on yourself. We are in this together. You did your best to hide it away, and you've kept it safe all this time. Now it's time we all protect it."

"Why didn't I destroy it?" I ask.

Langston shifts in his seat. "Maybe you did?"

I rack my brain, but I don't have a clue. "Well, unfortunately, we won't know until we find the box and confirm it still exists."

"Time is running out, Ren," Langston says, taking my hand in his.

A knock at the door startles us. It looks like time has already run out.

23

ZEKE

I NEVER EXPECTED to be at Langston's place so soon, yet here I am, standing tied up in the doorway while Julian knocks on the door. Six men stand behind us with guns pointed at me to keep me in check.

The door opens, and Langston stands in the doorway.

"I'm surprised to see you here. This wasn't part of the plan," Langston says to Julian.

"Plans change, you know that. Are you going to invite us in?"

"You and Zeke sure, but I don't need my house overrun by your calvary."

Julian frowns. "My men stay with me."

"Why? Don't you trust me? My security system is the best in the world."

Julian steps inside, pushing Langston out of the way, before snapping his fingers at his men to follow. Two of his men shove me inside, not that they need to. Siren is inside. I need to see her.

Langston gets in Julian's face. "Your men can stay in the front of the house. The rear is off-limits."

"Fine," Julian says, grabbing my ropes and pulling me after him as we walk into the living room.

I see Siren—similarly tied up. She's still wearing an oversized sweatshirt to hide her growing belly. Her legs and arms are tied to the chair she's sitting in, and her mouth is taped shut.

I look at Langston and growl through the bandana tied around my mouth. *Why did he have to tie her up? Why use tape on her mouth?*

He glares back, not giving away whose side he is on at all.

I turn my attention back to Siren. She doesn't look hurt. I don't see any visible bruises or scars. There isn't even a mark on her cheek from when Langston slapped her face.

She's fine, I tell myself.

Julian yanks on my ropes as he takes a seat on the couch. Langston sits opposite him, while I continue to stand. Both men ignore Siren and me.

"I came here because I need to speak with Siren alone," Julian says.

Langston laughs, crossing his leg over his knee as he leans back. "No. I have my prisoner. You have yours. That's how this works."

"Except, Siren isn't your prisoner. I already bought her months ago," Julian says.

"Actually, I bought her months ago," Langston says.

"And you sold her. She wasn't yours to buy. She has always been mine. Maybe not physically, but her life belongs to me."

"What does that mean?" Langston leans forward in his chair.

"She traded the rest of her life for Zeke's when she saved him from the water and brought her to me. She's mine. She has no choice but to tell me where the box is. Otherwise, I'll take Zeke's life."

Siren's eyes widen, and she fights against the constraints.

Shhh, baby, it will be okay. If anyone is going to die, it should be me, not you.

Langston looks from Julian to me. He doesn't know how to get out of this.

I tear the bandana from my mouth with my teeth. "I'll take her debt."

Julian looks at me with a smirk. "Do you realize what you are offering?"

"Yes, I'll take Siren's place."

"You are offering to be my loyal servant for the rest of your life?"

I gasp and look at Siren. I didn't realize she had promised Julian her life in order to save mine.

"Yes," I say.

"Then it looks like Siren is my prisoner. And Zeke is yours," Langston says.

Julian frowns, and I can tell he isn't sure he likes the trade.

"Regardless who belongs to whom, you and I have a deal. Together, we need to find that box, and she is the only one who knows where it is," Julian says, staring at Siren sadistically.

"Don't worry. I'll make her talk," Langston says.

"You have until morning to make her talk. Otherwise, it's my turn to try," Julian says with a smirk.

Langston nods in agreement.

Fuck.

Langston walks over to Siren and rips the tape holding her to the chair from her ankles and legs, before twisting her arms behind her back, forcing her to stand, and leading her away.

Langston brushes her hair off her neck and then puts his lips on my woman. I buck against my restraints trying to get to her, but Julian holds me back.

"I'm going to enjoy making you talk," Langston says against her neck.

I lose it. I run at Langston, but three of Julian's men quickly tackle me to the ground.

Langston and Julian both chuckle.

"Come, my beauty." Langston pulls on Siren's wrist. She fights him gently, not really struggling as hard as she can.

Langston isn't going to hurt her. He's on our side.

Langston and Siren disappear down the hallway to his bedroom. I wince when I hear a thump and a light scream.

Julian notices my reaction. "Don't worry, Bishop is a gentle man underneath all that hard exterior. Tonight, she'll sleep easily. Tomorrow is when the real pain begins."

Julian heads down the hallway to one of the spare bedrooms.

His men tie me up in the chair Siren had just occupied, and then make beds for themselves on the couches and floor.

A man to my left starts snoring almost immediately, but it's a welcome sound. It drowns out a little of the screaming, yelping, and whimpering coming from down the hallway.

It's all fake, I repeat to myself.

But what if it isn't?

———

"Zeke."

165

The voice jolts me awake, and I almost yell, I'm awoken so abruptly with a hand over my mouth.

"Shh, come on," Langston says.

My eyes widen when I realize Langston is standing in front of me. I look down and see that my hands and ankles have become untied.

Langston motions with his head to follow him, so I do. The men in the living room sleep soundly as we tiptoe away. We continue toward the open back door and then outside into the garden out back.

Siren is sitting on the edge of a fountain, waiting for me. When she sees me, she jumps up and runs toward me.

Our arms tangle around each other as soon as we reach each other. If I have it my way, we will never let go again.

"I was so afraid that Julian killed you," Siren cries into my shoulder.

"Never. You know that bastard can't take me down."

I glance behind me and realize that Langston has disappeared. Hopefully, he's standing guard, so Siren and I can have a few moments together.

And I'm going to make the most of every second we have together.

I grab the hem of her sweatshirt and lift it over her head. She's wearing a tank top underneath, and I lift that next. She's not wearing a bra, so I can see every bit of her under the moonlight.

I run my hands down her arms, then across her chest, and finally over her stomach. I turn her around and then run my hand over her smooth back. There isn't a mark on her body.

Finally, I turn her back to me.

"Satisfied?" Siren asks.

"Yes."

"Langston didn't touch me. He protected me."

"Thank God for that." I grab her cheeks and pull her lips to mine so I can kiss her like I want to. Her arms go under my shirt, feeling me over to check that I'm all in one piece too.

"Satisfied?" I ask with a smirk.

"Yes," she breathes.

"God, I need you, Siren. I'm not going to be able to sleep tonight without fucking you first."

She bites her lip. "Neither will I."

There aren't many places to fuck in the garden. I wish we had a bed or even a shower. But all we have is a garden of flowers, a fountain, and a small bench.

I grab her hand and pull her toward the bench, but when I sit down on the bench to pull her into my lap, it creaks. There is no way we are going to sit, let alone fuck on it, without breaking the small wooden thing.

Siren laughs. "Come here." She pulls my hand, and I stand and follow Siren as she leads me through the garden to a small patch of grass. Then she yanks me down to the grass with her.

I laugh along with her as I situate myself on my elbows over her.

"I feel like a kid again," she says.

"You'll feel all woman once I get done with you."

Her eyes light up at my words before I reach between her legs and rub her gently. Her eyes roll back, and her body writhes beneath me as I rub over her pants. I can feel her growing wetter.

"Zeke, fuck me, please."

I pull her pants down and slip my finger between her folds.

"So wet, so ready."

"Yes," she breathes.

She fumbles with my jeans, trying to get the button and zipper undone as quickly as possible. I understand her need to move quickly. Time has been taken from us too many times. There is never a guarantee that we will have more than a few minutes together. Never a guarantee of more time than the present.

I shove my jeans down as soon as she gets the button undone, and then she's pulling me toward her wet entrance. My cock doesn't need guidance—inside her is all it ever wants. I could find her with my eyes closed, and all my senses turned off.

I push her thighs back, spreading her wider as I push into her.

She gasps as I fill her.

"I remember you," she says suddenly.

"Did you ever forget me?"

She grins. "I forgot our first meeting in the bar when I sat on your lap."

I thrust in and out of her until she's unable to speak, too focused on how incredible she feels.

It gives me a moment to study her. To let my heart fill. To remember all my moments with her. *How could I ever forget?*

"Fuck me, my beast-man."

I grin wildly, remembering her sitting on my lap and calling me her beast-man, even then. I remember her flirting with me.

"You kissed me that night. That was our first kiss."

"I did not," she breathes again as I slow my thrusts.

I wait for her to remember.

"Oh my god! I did kiss you." She bites her lip, remembering that delicious kiss. We didn't know each other at all.

It was just an instant connection. We both knew that the moment wouldn't last, but one day we would be together again. We needed one sweet moment to take with us forever.

I bite her bottom lip, pulling it into my mouth like she did to me when we kissed the first time.

Her eyes meet mine. She remembers.

I grab her hips, and she tugs my neck holding me close to her. I thrust in and out. Over, and over, circling her clit with my groin, until she's ready to scream my name and I hers.

I crash my mouth over hers to muffle our screams as we both come together. I spill into her as she clenches down on me.

We stay locked together for a moment, knowing this could be the last time.

"It won't be," I say, reading her mind.

"No, our forever has to last a lot longer than this." She kisses my wedding ring.

I nod and help her off the grass before we both get dressed again. And then I pull her onto my lap as we sit and relax, our time together fleeting.

"How close are you to remembering?" I ask.

"That's as much as I've remembered. I killed my parents just after I hid the box, so Langston and I both think I need to experience a similar trauma in order to trigger the memory. We found a rapist and killed him, but it barely triggered anything."

Siren is silent after she speaks, fidgeting with the strands of her hair as she pulls a piece of grass out of it.

"What aren't you telling me?"

Her eyes look behind me, and that's when I spot Langston standing over us.

"She didn't remember after killing the rapist was because the violence wasn't personal. She didn't know the man. She needs to kill someone she knows and loves. Someone like me," Langston says, with his hands in the pocket of his jeans.

I look from Siren to Langston. "You can't kill him."

"She wouldn't have to actually kill me. Just make her think she did. Stop just short of killing me," Langston says.

I'm still having a hard time forgiving Langston for what he did before. But offering to let Siren almost kill him, knowing that it could result in his actual death, washes the slate clean instantly.

"You can't kill him," I repeat again, and I feel Siren relax in my arms. It's clear she doesn't want to kill him either.

"You can't kill him because you are going to kill me instead," I say.

24

SIREN

"No."

I stand abruptly, removing my hands from his.

"I'm not asking you to actually kill me," Zeke.

"Then what are you suggesting?" I turn toward Zeke with fear and pain.

"Just that you could—almost kill me."

I frown. "No, it's too dangerous. What if you actually died?"

He shrugs. "Then, you'd be no worse off."

"No. I would be devastated, and I wouldn't recover."

His lips thin. "I know, but there isn't any other choice."

"You could kill me, instead," Langston offers again.

"No, I'm not killing anyone," I say.

Zeke grabs my arms and forces me to look at him. "You won't kill me. We will make sure of it. We'll put fail-safes in place. Trust me. Langston will be here to ensure you don't kill me. But we have to find the box. Julian will torture you to get the information if we don't find it tonight."

I exhale my stress. "What is your plan?"

He reaches around me and pulls my gun from my waist. "Well, I won't let you shoot me again."

"I second that," Langston says.

I laugh, giving them the reaction they were hoping for.

But Zeke's own smile falters. "Drown me."

"What? No—"

He nods. "Drown me. It's personal and physical, but even if you go too far, there is a good chance you can bring me back. You know CPR?"

"Yes."

"And there is AED in the hall," Langston says. He jogs off to go get what we might need.

"I don't like this," I say.

"I don't really either, but we are out of time."

I don't know what to say.

Zeke grabs my hand and starts leading me toward the fountain.

Jesus Christ. I can't do this.

But Zeke looks at me with so much determination. He's willing to do anything to help me remember. I can't just say no. If I ever doubted Zeke's love for me, I can't anymore.

I can't doubt Langston's either. He was just as willing to die for me.

Langston sets supplies down next to the fountain—a towel, the AED, and rope. And then he looks at Zeke. "It should be me."

"No, it should be me. She loves you. I can see that, but Siren and I share a deeper love. If anyone is going to trigger her memories, it's going to be me."

I frown at the rope Langston picks up.

Zeke pulls off his shirt, and as much as I want to take in his muscles and run my hands over them, I'm too focused on what I'm about to do.

Langston hands me the rope as Zeke turns around and puts his arms behind his back.

"Tie them together, Siren."

"I can't. Can't Langston do it?"

Langston steps back, out of view. He won't help me with any part but making sure that Zeke doesn't die. That's his role. My role is to carry out every bit of the violence, to remember.

"I'll do my best not to fight you until I can't stand it any longer. But if you don't tie me up, I'll fight too soon, and you won't feel like you are actually killing me," Zeke says.

"This is outrageous," I protest, but I tie his arms together.

Zeke kneels in front of the fountain. I stand frozen behind him.

"Siren, please."

I step forward, my arms and legs shaking. My mother's face flashes in my head. Water comes next.

More flashes of memories flow.

Blood.

Tears.

Please...

The memories move me forward; I need to try this. This could be what helps me remember.

I walk up behind Zeke, reluctantly, just like I did when I was killing my own mother.

I push Zeke's head down, until it's submerged in the water. And then I hold him there, forcefully.

At first, not much happens.

It's peaceful.

I focus on the water—the moonlight shining down on me. I let my fear spread.

I have to do this.

Suddenly, then everything changes.

Zeke starts thrashing his head. Bubbles pour out of his mouth. It takes all of my strength to hold him under.

"MOTHER," I gasp, as her face comes into view.

"Please, don't kill me."

"I don't want to. But I can't let you have the box. Do you understand what it contains? What power it wields?" Please say no. Please say that you didn't realize, that you don't want it.

"Yes. The world needs to be rid of monsters. This is the only way to erase half the world. To get rid of the evil."

"By unleashing uncontrollable evil onto the world?"

"We can control it. We have the cure. We will be able to give the cure to those deserving."

"No, you don't get to play God. You don't get to decide who lives and dies."

"What did you do with the box, Aria?"

"I hid it."

"Where?"

I shake my head. "Please, don't make me do this. Please, surrender. Give up. Let me save you."

"Give me the box, Aria." My mother attacks, running full force over me.

I move out of the way at the last second; it's too late for her momentum to stop her, she goes overboard into the water. I jump in after her, knowing what I have to do. She can't come back up. She has to stay under.

"SIREN! STOP!"

I blink rapidly as Langston yanks me away from the fountain and grabs Zeke's lifeless body.

"Oh my god!"

"Shh," Langston hushes me. He grabs a knife and swiftly rips through the rope tying Zeke's hands together. Then he puts Zeke on his back and begins chest compressions.

"Get the AED ready," Langston says.

I tear my eyes away from Zeke, who is lying lifeless on the ground. I open the AED box, pull out the application pads, and press them to Zeke's chest while Langston breathes a breath into Zeke's mouth.

The AED machine starts. "No heartbeat detected," the robot voice says.

"No, please, no," I say.

Langston grabs me and pulls me away from Zeke's body before the AED delivers a shock.

"Continue chest compressions," the robot guides us.

Langston restarts chest compressions, and I move to Zeke's head. "Breathe, Zeke. Come back to me. I need you. Come back."

The machine starts up again, telling us to step back.

We stop touching Zeke so the machine can deliver another shock.

"No heartbeat detected, continue chest compressions."

Langston continues.

"Zeke, please!"

Another zap from the machine, more chest compressions.

"I'm so sorry." I grab Zeke's head, breathing air into his mouth, hoping something will bring him back.

"No heartbeat detected."

The machine shocks him again. And then shuts off.

The machine has given up, but there is no way I'm giving up. I can't have killed him. This can't be happening.

I push Langston out of the way and pump down over his heart with all of my weight. I'm cracking ribs and crushing him, but I'll do anything to get his heart started again, including trading my soul to the devil if he will save him.

"Please," I beg to the silent night. "Don't let him die."

And then...I feel something—a fluttering of his heart beneath my hands.

"Yes, come on, Zeke. Wake up. Come back to me."

I continue doing hard compressions, while Langston breathes into Zeke's mouth.

Then, Zeke coughs.

He coughs!

He's alive.

I stop suddenly as he coughs up what looks like a gallon of water before falling back to the ground, exhausted.

"You are alive," I say through my tears.

Zeke's wipes my cheek dry with his thumb with a soft smile. "I couldn't stand Langston giving me anymore mouth to mouth. I would have thought you would be the one to do that, Siren."

I collapse on top of him, hugging him tightly.

"I'm so sorry," I cry into his chest.

He strokes my back. "Shh, I'm okay. You didn't do anything wrong."

I see tears in Langston's eyes when I look up. He was just as worried that he had killed his friend. He looks away, though, when he notices me staring.

How could I have ever thought that Langston was a bad man?

I focus back on Zeke. "I'm just so thankful that you are alive. Your heart stopped, and we didn't think we could get it started again."

Zeke holds my cheeks in his hands, wiping my tears

with his thumbs and tucking my hair behind my ears, trying to comfort me.

"My heart will always beat for you."

I smile through the tears as I try to catch my breath.

Zeke takes a deep breath, and I realize I'm squashing him. I roll off him and help him sit up.

"How are you feeling?" I ask.

"Like the luckiest man in the world to be married to you."

"Seriously, how does your chest feel?"

He takes a deep breath in and out. "It burns a little, but I can get a good breath, so I think I'll be fine."

I nod.

"I hate to end this, but we should get back soon before any of the men start waking up," Langston says, and then he starts walking back toward the house to give us a chance to say goodbye once again.

"I'm so tired of saying goodbye," I say.

"This isn't goodbye. We are together, now. I'm not letting anything stand between us. Not again." Zeke leans down and presses his lips to mine. I return the kiss fiercely. We don't let our tongues slip into each other's mouths; we just seal our lips together like we've become one person.

Slowly, Zeke pulls us apart. As much as he says we will be together, that this isn't goodbye, my heart can no longer escape the dreaded feeling.

"Did it work?" Zeke asks.

"What?" I ask, not understanding his question.

"Did your memories come back?" he asks.

My mother flashes in my head. She came back, but nothing else. I still don't remember where the box is. There is nothing Zeke can do about it now, though. He won't let us go back inside if he thinks I don't remember, and we have to go back inside. If we run, Julian will hunt us down and kill us. We aren't running, not anymore. We will face this, now.

"Yes," I say. It's the truth—I do remember. But it is also the most horrible sin, because I don't remember the important part—where the box is.

Zeke nods. "Good." He kisses my temple.

He takes my hand and leads me back to the house, where Langston is standing guard. I notice Langston has a roll of tape in his hands, reminding us that Zeke has to be tied up again, while I will be sleeping in Langston's room.

I quickly kiss Zeke one last time. I keep it short; otherwise, I wouldn't stop kissing him.

"Ready?" Langston asks us.

We nod and silently follow him into the house.

Zeke holds my hand for as long as he can before he has to take a seat again. Langston reties Zeke to the chair, none of us speaking for fear of waking up the sleeping guards.

Zeke winks at me with a wicked sultry grin, and I bite my lip and blush in return.

Once Zeke is retied, Langston walks over to me. He gives me a stern look that tells me we have to go, but I can't get my feet to move.

Langston tugs on my hand, but I'm frozen, watching Zeke.

Eventually, Langston picks me up and carries me down the hallway, away from Zeke.

Once in the bedroom, Langston locks the door and sets me down on the bed before he sits next to me.

"Did you really remember?"

"I remembered my mother, but not where I hid the box."

Langston takes my hand in his, trying to comfort me as he rubs his thumb over the back of my hand.

"What are we going to do?" I ask.

"We will think of something. I won't let Julian hurt you; I promise you that."

We sit on the edge of the bed in silence for a while. We should be sleeping.

Suddenly, out of nowhere, Langston slaps me.

I turn and look at him as I grab my cheek, more from shock than pain.

"What are you doing?"

There is no remorse in his eyes. No apology. And no reason for this that I can see.

He grabs me by the arm with such force I'm sure he's going to bruise me and throws me back on the bed. He ties me up roughly while I'm lying on my back, still in too much shock to fight back.

He takes a piece of tape and moves to put it over my mouth.

"I thought you were my friend. Why are you doing this?"

He puts the tape on my mouth, silencing me.

"The truth is I was never your friend. I just pretended to be to get what Julian wanted. I'm on Julian's side. I'm a monster." Langston walks to the bathroom, while I lay in bed tied up. A single tear rolls down my cheek.

How could I have been so wrong about Langston? He really is Bishop. He really is a monster.

25

ZEKE

SOMEHOW I SLEEP, even though my lungs burn from being filled with water.

I've never been so terrified in my life. I've been near death before; that isn't what had me panicked. What I feared was that Siren would kill me, and then she'd never forgive herself.

Siren brought me back to life even after I was dead, but my body is paying the price for it. Even though I'm tied up in a chair and in a ton of pain, I was able to sleep because my body demanded it.

However, the noise coming down the hallway is what woke me up.

Julian marched toward Langston and Siren's room, and as soon as he started down that hallway, the sounds started up again from Langston's room—smacking, yelping, crying.

I tried to block it out. It's not real; I saw it all before. They did this dance earlier, and I got to see Siren after. She didn't have a mark on her. I hope they find a way to make her look beat up without having to mark her at all. Julian will know something is up if she comes out looking untouched.

That must be what they are doing now.

Please, be careful. Don't really hurt her.

Julian knocks on the bedroom door. "Time's up. We need to talk."

He then walks into the living room; his men wake to attention.

The noises coming from their bedroom quiet for a minute, and then Langston appears, dragging Siren behind him by the hair.

I come unglued. She looks a disheveled mess. Her clothes and hair are all awry. Most of her clothes are heavily torn, revealing bruises and scratches.

They aren't real. Or if they are real, they are mild. Just enough necessary to make it appear that Langston raped and tortured her all night.

But there are tears in her eyes. Real. Genuine. Tears.

I fight against my restraints. *Damn Langston for taping my arms and legs so tightly that I can't break free.*

It's not real. She's acting.

Jesus, does it look real.

Langston releases Siren, and she scoots away to the corner of the room like she's terrified of him. She's not tied up, cowering in the corner against the wall.

What the hell is happening? What did I miss?

"Where is it?" Julian sits in one of the chairs, motioning for Langston to sit opposite of him.

"Scotland," Langston answers, naming a country and not a specific place.

Julian narrows his eyes. "Where exactly?"

Langston doesn't answer. *Does he not know? Did Siren*

keep the information to herself? Or does he not want to tell Julian?

"Fine, don't tell me. I'll make her tell me," Julian stands and moves toward Siren.

Fight, baby. Kick his ass.

She doesn't move, though. She slumps to the floor, practically curling into a ball, so unlike my Siren.

I fight against my restraints, but I make no progress.

Julian goes to grab Siren's hair, but Langston grabs his wrist.

"She's mine. Until we have the box, she's my assurance that you won't betray me. I know you want her," Langston says, throwing Julian's hand down.

Julian studies Siren closer, and I see the secret revealed a second before he does, but it's too late.

"You're pregnant?" Julian says, blinking at Siren.

She stares down at the floor, not looking at him.

"Answer me! Are. You. Pregnant?"

Siren finally looks up at him, the heat and fire returning to her eyes. "Yes."

"Whose? Whose is it?"

Julian studies her belly, like it holds all the answers, like it can tell him whose baby she's caring.

I fight the scarf off from around my mouth. "MINE," I growl.

Everyone's attention turns to me when I speak.

Julian turns to me. "How do you know for sure? I raped her several weeks ago. It would make sense if the baby were mine."

There is a small chance the baby is his, but I'm not letting him know that. He will never be a father. I will ensure that.

"We had a DNA test run to ensure I was the father. If

not, Siren was going to terminate the pregnancy." It's a lie, but I don't care. I don't want Julian to have any claim to the baby. Siren assured me she doesn't think it's him. She's too far along for it to be his. But I want him to know definitively that the baby isn't his.

Julian's reaction is blank. He doesn't blink, and he doesn't show emotion on his face. Instead, he walks into the kitchen and then returns a moment later with a roll of tape.

I snarl at him as he takes a piece of tape and wraps it over my mouth, assuring my silence.

"I'll find out if the baby is mine or not. If it's mine, I will enjoy raising it with Siren. If it's not, I will destroy it."

I fight so hard that I break the chair I'm sitting in. I've never wanted to kill a man more than I do now. The second I get my legs free, five men dive on top of me. They quickly tie more ropes around me and hold me down, taking two men per rope to ensure I'm immobile.

He threatened my child. I'm going to kill him and then bring him back to life and kill him again, over and over.

Julian's phone buzzes, and he frowns before looking at it. He answers, "Yes."

There's a pause.

"We're close."

Another pause.

"I understand."

And then he ends the call. He looks to Langston. "Where exactly is it located?"

"All I've gotten is a country. But if I spend the day with her, I'm sure I'll get the exact location," Langston says. "Why don't you head to Scotland, and we will follow as soon as I finish breaking her."

"No, we are out of time. It has to be today. Get her to tell us now, or I will."

Langston looks like he wants to object, but decides against it. I plead with him with my eyes to save Siren. I don't care about me. Just get her and get out of here. I'll find a way to kill Julian. We can hunt his financier down after Julian is dead.

Langston walks over to Siren, who coils back like he's about to strike out at her. Her reaction terrifies me.

He grabs one of her wrists and starts dragging her to his bedroom.

Julian sits down in his chair and flicks on the TV as Langston leaves. Then Julian flicks the channel to Langston's security system.

"Put on a good show," Julian says, winking at Langston as he drags Siren out of the room.

Fuck.

I give Langston one last plea with my eyes. *You can escape. Take Siren out the window and make a run for it. Kai and Enzo will be here soon to help me. Just save her.* There is no way to fake torturing her on a live feed. And I know Siren, she won't give up the location when she knows Julian is listening.

Langston gives me no indication of what he's thinking as he drags Siren down the hallway away from me once again.

I stare at the TV, waiting for them to come back into view. I take in the wrecked room on the screen. The comforter and sheets are half on the bed. The furniture is all messed up with drawers out, and lamps thrown to the floor.

Please don't let any more damage happen. Please let Siren and our baby be okay.

Langston and Siren come back into view. She tries to pull away and get him to let go of her wrists, but the way he's gripping her wrist, there is no way her arm can slip through.

"Let me go!" Siren cries, her legs are kicking against Langston to let her go.

Langston ignores her pleas, her suffering. The pain she's trying to inflict on him doesn't even phase him.

Siren pulls hard on his grip, throwing her entire body to the floor to try and make it as difficult as possible for Langston.

I know my girl; she can escape any man. If Langston is truly hurting her, Siren will fight back until she escapes.

This is all fake, a show.

Langston drags her through the room to the bed.

Do not get in that bed.

Then he's yanking her up by her wrists and throwing her into the bed.

Siren immediately tries to roll off the other side of the bed, but Langston grabs her ankle and yanks her back. He throws his weight on top of her, pinning her body underneath him.

Julian snickers next to me.

I scream beneath the tape over my mouth. I don't understand how he is okay with another man raping a woman who he feels is his.

Julian looks at me and laughs. "Don't worry, Zeke. She's not Bishop's. He's just borrowing her. She's *mine*."

I fight harder against my restraints and yell through the tape, hoping Julian will want to talk and remove the tape, but his eyes have turned back to the screen. Mine follow, although I wish they hadn't—because what I see will never leave my mind. Not ever.

Siren's pants are around her ankles. Her wrists are

pinned together in one of Langston's hands above her head, and his body is pressed between her legs.

I can't watch this, even if it's fake, but I can't tear my eyes away from it either. I'm trapped in a horror movie.

There is no audio from the security camera; the only sounds we hear are when Langston makes her scream or cry loud enough that we can hear down the hallway.

We can't see their mouths move at this angle either, so I don't know if they are talking. I don't know what sounds Siren is making.

Langston's hand roars back, and there's a slap.

"Hit the bitch again!" one of the guards shouts at the TV.

"Strip her and turn her around so we can see her. This is better than free porn," another guard says, and then they are all chuckling together, shouting out what they want Langston to do to her like they are watching an HBO fight or something.

Come on, baby. Kick him off you. Do something. Show me you still have some fight left in you.

Then I see a knife that Langston has pulled out and pushed against her neck. She's breathing heavily but doesn't move. Her eyes dart down, trying to get a look at how he's holding the knife to her neck, but otherwise, she's as still as stone.

This is fake, I repeat to myself for the thousandth time. This is just an orchestrated dance to please Julian. This is just so Langston can still pretend he is working with Julian; so that he can get close to him and eventually help us kill him.

But the way he's holding the knife against her carotid has me nervous. He's pressing harder than necessary. It seems real, so fucking real.

Make up a lie about where the box is, and end this—please.

I watch carefully, every movement.

Langston continues to hold the knife to her neck as he reaches down and works on his pants.

My eyes widen, watching in fear.

This is fake.

Fake.

Fake.

Fake.

He's not going to rape her. He's not going to hurt her.

A single tear drops from Siren's eye, landing in the corner. She looks disgusted at Langston, like she hates him worse than any man she's ever hated.

Siren hates Julian. He raped her, violated her. But I know that thinking about me saved her from the pain.

She's not thinking about me, now. She's hating Langston —a man who she thought was her friend. Who I believed was my friend.

"No!" I scream through the tape as I watch him position himself between her legs, keeping the knife at her neck, her hands stay above her head, likely because he's told her he'll slit her throat if she moves.

Julian's eyes darken.

The room quiets as they watch with fascination.

And then I watch him thrust his hips.

I watch her cringe in disgust.

That single tear that was caught in her eye rolls down her cheek and off her chin.

That tear tells me everything—this is real.

This isn't fake.

Langston played us both.

He's not our friend.

He works for Julian.

From the smug expression on Julian's face, this is why he was willing to let Langston rape Siren. He wanted to show me, once and for all, whose side Langston is on—his. Julian won the war. He got Siren. And he turned my best friend against me.

I fight with all my might against the bindings, but I can't break free. I'm locked where I am with nothing to look at, but my beautiful wife being violated.

I feel bile rising in my throat. I'd vomit if there wasn't tape covering my mouth.

I'm going to kill him.

I'm going to kill them all—burn everyone in this house, send them all to hell.

I watch Langton thrust into Siren like she's his, like he has the right. No one has the right.

I failed.

I failed to protect her.

This is my biggest failure. The only reason she's with Langston right now is because I told her to trust him. I thought he was my friend. I was so wrong.

I will never forgive myself.

But I can't keep letting this go on. I have to stop it. *I have to.*

I fight harder, pushing again and again and again against the bindings. I get one ankle free then the other.

The men are too focused on the TV to notice.

I pull hard on my wrists, but I can't get them free.

I stare at the TV, gaining strength from Siren to save her. Siren must have decided this is the moment to fight back, too, because I see her and Langston struggling instead of him thrusting.

Yes, we have to fight back. We won't take this without fighting. Together, we are going to destroy them all.

I rip my arms free and then rip the tape from my mouth. This gets everyone's attention, but it's too late. Nothing will stop me from running into the room, ripping Langston off of Siren, and squeezing the life out of Langston.

A guard comes at me, but I punch him, knocking him down with one hit.

Two more attack from the side with guns firing at me. I dodge the bullets, grab a gun from one of them and use it to fire at the other before turning it on the other guard. Both men drop.

Then I turn and fire the gun at the other three men. I move to turn the gun on Julian when he gasps at the sight on the TV before shouting, "You're a fucking dead man!"

He starts storming down the hallway before I have a chance to fire at him.

I glance at the TV, scared of what I will find.

Blood.

So much fucking blood covers the white sheet, droves and droves of blood. Langston continues to lie on top of Siren, so I can't figure out where the blood is coming from on the TV.

The sight only amplifies my speed. I run down the hallway, knocking Julian aside so I can be the first to burst through the room.

The moment in front of me almost makes me faint. I've never seen anything worse; nothing could be worse.

Siren dead is the only imaginable thing that could be worse.

The blood I see is unimaginable.

I can't tell where it's coming from.

I grab Langston by the back of his neck and throw him off of her. I have to get to her. I have to end her pain. I have to protect her from any more evil.

When I rip him off her, I see where the blood is coming from—from between her legs. I look over at Langston, who has pulled his pants up, blood all over him as well.

I look back at Siren with so many tears and pain in my eyes. I can't breathe. I can't think. My heart stops. And unlike last time, I don't think it can be resuscitated. It will never work properly again.

What I see can't be true. I can't have let this happen. I can't have.

I open my mouth to ask, but my voice doesn't work, only my tears.

My tears fall freely, pouring gallons of water out of my eyes. My very soul escapes through my tear ducts.

The pain I see on Siren's face isn't physical. It's not because Langton physically hurt her. It's because of what she knows is true, the loss she's experiencing.

I open my mouth again, my lungs still burning from being drowned, but now my throat has tightened, making it almost impossible to speak. But I have to; I have to know the truth, no matter how painful, how horrible, how unthinkable. I have to face it. I have to be strong for her.

I hear Julian behind me. Langston is moving toward us. I need a moment to understand that truth. After that, I'll turn into the monster I need to be to destroy the men behind me. But right now, I need to connect Siren and my's pain. I need it to fuel me through my heartache and make the men pay who did this.

I take Siren's hand in mine through our tears, and then I push through my pain.

"The baby?" I ask above barely a whisper.

Siren purses her lips, letting all the air out of her body, like that will somehow let the truth out, but it doesn't. She has to speak. She has to tell me.

"Gone," she yelps as she says it, like speaking the truth makes it true.

My head drops to hers as our pain mixes. Our hearts break. I don't know how we survive this pain. I don't know how Siren can ever forgive me for letting this happen.

But I know that I will make every man responsible pay.

26

SIREN

GONE—THE word burns through me. Just like the pain. I never thought I'd experience such trauma, such loss. But here I am, experiencing the worst thing possible.

Zeke's head rests against my forehead. The pain flows through him as powerfully as water over rapids. I feel every sharp intake of his breath, every rip of his heart, every vibration of his pain. I sense it all.

I feel his pain worse than I feel my own. It's intolerable to him. He won't recover from this. The man I knew is gone. I've destroyed him with my news.

My truth.

My sinful truth.

I close my eyes, and I remember. The trauma, the worst trauma I can imagine short of Zeke dying, is what spirals me into the past. What causes me to remember everything. All the truths I've hidden.

I WALK UP the large hill completely out of breath. I look behind me, afraid I'm being tracked, but of course, I'm not. Everyone who knows about this is either dead or thinks the fake I swapped it with is real. There is no one coming after me. At least, not yet.

But someday, I know they will. A great evil will come for it. And when that happens, I will have this box as hidden as humanly possible.

So I keep climbing, even though I'm exhausted. My feet burn, my heart aches with the pain I've endured to protect the box. This is my destiny; this is my purpose—to protect the world from this danger.

Finally, I step foot on top of the large hill. An old fashioned castle straight out of the fourteenth century sits on top. I take a deep breath.

I'm doing the right thing.

I walk to the door, and before I have a chance to knock, a man opens it. A man I've never met before but who I instantly trust.

"Are you sure you want to hide it, instead of destroying it?" he asks me, not even giving me an introduction. He knows why I'm here, and he knows that finishing the task is more important than small talk.

"Yes, I can't say exactly why. Mostly a feeling that it's going to be needed someday."

He nods. "You don't have to explain it to me. You are the one who should make the decision. I trust you."

I pull the box out of my bag and hold it out to him. "Just as I trust you."

He takes it from me. "I'll guard it with my life."

"Even from me?"

He hesitates but then finally agrees. "Yes, I'll guard it, even from you."

"Thank you. I know what I'm asking."

"Nothing more than is required."

He doesn't invite me in. Even if he did, I can't come inside. I *need to leave. I need to forget. I need to finish my task and figure out how I can forget, so no one can ever use me to find such evil.*

"I should go."

"I would say until next time, but if we did this right, we will never meet again," he says.

That saddens me, that I'll never get to know this man. But it's for the best. He's the only person I feel I can trust. And I don't have anything to say. There is nothing I can say. I have to leave. I can't communicate with him. I can't come back here. Even to step foot in this country would be putting the world at risk.

But I can't bring myself to say goodbye either. Instead, I turn, and I walk down the hill, away from the only family I have left.

I OPEN my eyes and find Zeke staring at me.

"Baby?" he asks, trying to understand what just happened to me. He thinks I already knew the location of the box, so I shouldn't tell him I didn't know until just now.

Instead, I just bite my lip, like the pain I'm feeling is too much for me to bear. He pulls me into a hug, and then all hell breaks loose.

Gunshots ring out all around the room and house.

Zeke falls on top of me, shielding me with his body as the bullets fly.

My eyes cut under Zeke's arm to see to the door. "Kai and Enzo are here," I whisper to him.

"Don't trust Langston!" Zeke shouts to them.

A gun is tossed on the bed. Zeke grabs it and turns, keeping his body over mine as he starts firing at the men coming into the room. I don't know where all these men are coming from, but half work for Enzo and Kai, while the other half work for Julian, or at least Julian's financier.

Another loud boom rings out, causing Zeke to yank me

off the bed with him, and then use the bed as protection while he shoots over it.

"Stay behind me, no matter what, okay?" Zeke asks.

"Yes," I say.

"Let's go," Zeke says, when there is a break in the gunfire.

I peer around him and find only one man firing toward us from the door. I don't know where Langston or Julian went, or where Enzo or Kai went, but it appears the fighting has moved to another part of the house.

Zeke grabs my hand, and we move around the bed. Zeke kills the man at the door, and when we get to the door, he grabs a gun on the ground and hands it to me.

He gives me a warning look. *Stay behind him. Only fire when necessary. Stay safe.*

I nod. Then we are moving through the hallway. By the time we get to the living room, I realize that half the house has been blown away. It saddens me for a second to see such a beautiful house destroyed, but that thought is gone the next second as we come across the main fight.

Men are shooting everywhere, smoke billows around us, making it impossible to see clearly.

"There is a car in the garage. If we get separated, meet me there," Zeke says.

"Okay."

And then we push through, firing and slinking low through the smoke.

I cough as smoke enters my lungs, but I keep pressing on; I have to. We can't stay in this house much longer.

Zeke keeps moving forward, but I lose him.

There is more smoke toward the direction of the garage. I have to get out of the house before I head to the garage, or I won't be able to breathe much longer.

I end up crawling on all fours, searching for someone I trust.

I cough over and over. It burns, my eyes are watering, my nose dripping.

I collapse on the floor, unable to get enough oxygen to breathe. Gunshots ring out in the distance. Apparently, the battle has moved away from the smoke. I'd rather deal with a barrage of bullets than this thick smoke, too.

I start crawling again, unable to see my hands in front of me as I move. I have to keep going, though.

I consider calling for help, but I'm afraid it could draw the wrong attention of the wrong people. And from all my coughing, I probably wouldn't be able to yell very loudly anyway.

Must.

Move.

Forward.

I have to get out of the smoke. Of all the ways that I envisioned my death, dying in a house filled with smoke with people just outside who could save me, if they could just find me, was not the way that I thought I would go.

My head spins, and I start seeing spots.

I cough again as I try to suck in any oxygen, but there seems to be none left in the house.

I refuse to die like this. I will find a way through this even though my body is shutting down; my heartbeat is growing weaker; my chest has tightened.

I collapse, my arms are unable to move me forward any further. Maybe if I hover close to the ground, I'll be able to get enough oxygen until the smoke lifts.

So that's what I do while praying for a miracle.

"I got you." His voice is strong, despite the smoke. His

arms scoop me up, and then we are running through the smoke. I cough against his chest; he grips me tighter.

We are through the smoke a moment later, but he doesn't stop running. I suspect he won't until he gets us somewhere he deems safe.

I continue to cough as he runs for what seems like miles before he finally stops. He unlocks a car and then places me in the back.

"Take a deep breath. In and out, slowly. You're safe now. There is plenty of oxygen for you to breathe. Just take some deep, slow breaths."

I try, but cough.

"Try again," he says.

I do.

I wheeze, but I'm able to get more oxygen this time and only cough a tiny bit.

"Good, again."

I take another breath, then another. The pain in my lungs eases a little with every breath.

"We need to go," he says, hopping in the front seat and putting the car in drive.

"I—" I say, starting to tell him everything that needs to be said, but my voice is hoarse.

"Shhh, Siren. Don't speak. You can tell me once we get to the airport," Langston cuts me off.

I need to speak. I have so much to say, but after everything that happened, I'm too weak. Too weak to talk. Too weak to fight. So instead, I drift off to sleep.

27

ZEKE

"Siren!" I yell as I cough just outside the band of smoke that has filled the house. I don't know where all the smoke is coming from; there doesn't seem to be a fire.

"Siren!" I scream again at the top of my lungs, but that only makes me cough worse.

A bullet buzzes by my head, and I turn and fire. I have to stay alive so I can save her. I will not fail her again. I will not. *I can't...*

"Don't move," Julian says.

I look up and see that Julian has Kai in a headlock with a gun pointed at her.

Fuck.

Enzo runs up beside me. I look around at our small group, but I don't see Siren or Langston.

My heart races, thinking they could be together.

No.

I just saw Siren a minute ago. She'll make her way out through the smoke the same as I did. Hopefully, she's made it to the garage as is hiding, waiting for me to get to her.

And no one seems to know where Langston is. Right now, I have to focus on Kai, on saving her.

"Let her go," I say through a cough.

"I'd be willing to make a trade," Julian says.

I sigh and hold my hands up, dropping my gun. I turn to Enzo beside me. "Take Kai and find Siren. Keep her safe and away from all of this. Don't trust Langston."

Enzo nods at me.

I step forward while Enzo keeps his gun aimed at Julian. When I get close, Julian pushes Kai away and aims his gun at me.

Kai looks at me with such pain. "Go," I tell her.

She hesitates a second and then Enzo says, "Stingray, we have to go."

Kai gives me one last look, and then she runs off with Enzo.

Please go find Siren. Let her be safe.

"They aren't going to find Siren," Julian says to me.

"Siren will lead them to her."

He shakes his head. "Unlikely, since she isn't alone."

"What do you mean?" But my heart already knows. I know it isn't smart, but I have to know she isn't here. I take off to the house behind me. Somehow, most of the smoke is gone when I enter the house.

"Siren!" I yell as I step over fallen men. I run throughout the house, even back to the bedroom I found her in, but she's not there.

I run through the house again. *Please, be in the garage.* I open the back door and step into the garage.

"Siren!" I yell again, looking through the cars and under them for her. She's gone.

"I told you, he has her," Julian says from the doorway.

I turn with all of my rage and face him. "Tell him to

bring her back, or neither of you will find the box. Call him and tell him right now, or I'll kill you. The only reason I've kept you alive is because I know you aren't the one in charge. There is another man paying you, pulling all the strings. And I thought you could lead me to him, but I'll kill you now if you don't have Langston bring her back right now."

"I have no doubt that is true, but there is just one problem."

"Which is?"

"I want Bishop, or Langston, whatever his name is, dead too."

I blink rapidly.

"I want him dead for what he did to Siren."

I scoff. "You raped her too, you know. You're no better than him."

"You're right, I'm not. But he killed her child, possibly my child, and I won't forgive him for that. I want him dead. He knows that. We aren't working together anymore."

I frown.

"This is what I suggest. You help me find the box, and I'll help you ensure Siren is safe," Julian says.

"Not likely, since you've tried to kill her more than most."

"I'll tell you a truth. I could never kill Siren. I love her as much as you do."

"No one loves her more than me."

Julian shakes his head. "I get the box. You get Siren. Do we have a deal?"

"And what happens to Langston?"

"The first one to find him gets to kill him."

Julian holds out a gun to me, and I take it. Then he's

pulling out his phone. "We are going to need a private jet at the Bilbao airport immediately."

Julian hangs up and climbs into a speed car. I climb in after him.

We haven't agreed on anything, but he has a car and a jet. I need both to get to Siren since Langston hasn't returned my money yet.

"How are we going to know where to go once we get to Scotland?" I ask as Julian starts the car.

Julian's eyes narrow. "Because Siren isn't the only one who just got her memory back."

28

SIREN

I OPEN MY EYES. I sit up and take in my surroundings. I'm lying on a couch on a private jet, surrounded by oval windows that frame fluffy clouds we are already flying through.

"Careful, don't sit up too fast," Langston says as I start pushing myself up. I cough as soon as I do.

"Here, breathe through this," Langston holds up an oxygen mask to my face that I realize is strapped around my neck and must have fallen off my face. I take a couple of deep breaths, and my lungs feel a bit better, yet I still cough a few times before I settle. When I feel better, I remove the oxygen mask.

"Here." Langston holds out a cup of tea to me.

I take it and sip.

"How are you feeling?" Langston asks. He's sitting on the couch next to me, staring at me with such intensity.

I cough again. "My chest and throat hurt, but otherwise, my main feeling is guilt for betraying Zeke."

He nods and then coughs as well.

I frown, not realizing that he might have inhaled as much smoke as I did when he rescued me.

"How are you feeling?" I ask.

He coughs again before clearing his throat. "Like I ruined a friendship forever."

I want to reassure him that he and Zeke will one day heal their relationship, but after what we did, I doubt that it will come easily. I'm going to have my hands full making sure Zeke doesn't kill Langston the next time we see him.

So I don't say anything.

"You didn't have a choice, you know. You had to do it. You had to hurt him," Langston says, knowing that I'm beating myself up for what I did to Zeke.

"I know, but I still hate hurting him. I hate lying to him. I hate all of it. When this is over, I hope I never have to lie again."

"Someday soon that day will come."

We both sip our teas. Unspoken questions linger between us. *Was it worth it? Did I get the information I needed?*

"We need to go to Inverness," I say, letting Langston know it was worth it.

"I'll go tell the pilots."

Langston stands and walks to the front of the plane to discuss flight plans.

The weight of what I did crashes down upon me.

I watched Zeke break, fully and completely. Zeke is devastated because of what I did. He shattered into a million pieces before my very eyes because of what I let him think, because of what I did.

My anchor is broken. He's hurting, and I can't comfort him, not until this is all over. He will never be the same. I don't think I'm able to put the pieces back together.

Tears start falling again, and my cough returns. Zeke isn't the only one; I'm broken too.

Zeke holds a part of me, and I won't be whole until we are together again.

I feel arms going around me as I cry. I swear I feel his tears wet my shoulder, but I don't pull away from his chest to verify.

"I've got you until you can be with Zeke again."

I shake in Langston's arms.

"I've got you," he repeats again.

"I know. Thank you for protecting me, even when I didn't realize that was what you were doing."

"I'm sorry I had to hurt you at all. I'm so sorry. I wish I could have come up with something different, something easier, to protect you. But—"

I pull back and wipe my eyes. "No, you did the right thing. Just like I did to Zeke."

"Forgive me?" Langston asks.

"There is nothing to forgive. But I forgive you, if that's what you need to hear."

I hug him again. Zeke is my husband, but Langston has quickly become someone special in my life. I don't know how to label our relationship. It's not a friendship, not like Nora and me, and it's different than a brother and sister relationship. I can't think of a term, but I imagine it feels a lot like how Kai and Zeke feel. Because of what we've been through, because of our shared pain, we will forever be connected.

He smiles at me. "Thank you."

"How long will it take us to get to Inverness?"

"Eight hours."

"We will beat them all there. We will find where you buried the box. And we will destroy it before anyone else can get there. We have a good couple of hours head start. After it's destroyed, I will make sure you are safe, and then I will help Zeke, Enzo, and Kai kill Julian and his financier."

"I didn't bury it," I say behind my eyelashes.

"What did you do with it then?"

"I gave it to a man."

He frowns. "Who? A man you trusted? How could you ensure it was safe? How do you know that it's still there?"

"Because the man is my brother."

Langston's eyes widen. "You have a brother?"

"I didn't know it either. He's thirteen years older than me. He was out of the house before I was old enough to know him. He lived by himself, away from the world. His heart is like mine. He knew how important it was to keep it safe. It's still there in the castle with him."

"Okay, good. We will get the box from him, then."

"He won't give it to us."

"What do you mean? I thought he was your brother? You trusted him to protect it?"

"I did. I do. But he promised to protect it, even from me."

Langston sinks back, realizing what it's going to take me to get the box—fighting my own brother. My own blood. I may have never known him, but it's still going to hurt trying to defeat him.

"We will find a way," Langston says, as he stares down at my stomach where I'm rubbing it. He puts his hand over mine, and we watch as we both feel a kick.

"We always find a way."

29

ZEKE

I sit on the plane headed to Scotland.

I try not to think about everything that has happened.

My friend's betrayal.

My wife's suffering.

My child's death.

I wait for the tears to come, but they don't. The tears have vanished, and in their absence, I've hardened into a man capable of untold sin. My wrath will be felt throughout the world. I will not rest until every man who had a hand, no matter how small, in my child's death pays for his sins.

I've made a deal with the devil to keep Siren safe and ensure that Langston pays for what he did, but the devil will also die for his part.

I'm tired of playing games. Today, the world burns.

Julian is sitting at the front of the private jet, staring at his phone, while I sit in the back, as far away from him as I can get. Several of his men sit in between us.

But I'm tired of waiting and not knowing all the players. I want to know who the men are that I will be burning to the ground.

I get out of my seat and march to the front. If Julian's men were smart, they'd try to stop me, but they aren't the most intelligent bunch. They can't see a threat coming when they need to.

Julian doesn't seem to think of me as a threat either because he doesn't so much as blink when I walk over to him.

I grab him by the shoulders and throw him hard against the other side of the plane. His head bashes into the wall, and then I shove my arm against his throat, making it hard for him to breathe.

"Who finances you? I've seen your bank accounts. I know you are wealthy beyond imagination. Those stupid tasks you sent me on were nothing more than a game to you. You haven't made your billions from smuggling drugs and people. Who finances you?"

"You think I'll tell you, just like that?"

"If you don't want to die."

"I won't be dying." His eyes dart around the room to his men, who finally caught on and have their guns aimed at me.

I lean in close. "My child is dead. My wife broken. You think I care about dying right now? I only care about wiping the earth of evil."

"Thomas, get us two whiskeys," Julian snaps at one of his men.

I narrow my eyes. "What are you doing?"

"We have a partnership. You want to talk? Let's talk."

The man brings over two whiskey glasses.

Julian raises his eyebrows, waiting for me to decide how to handle this.

I let him go and grab one of the glasses.

"Everyone out," Julian says.

The man who brought us the glasses directs everyone to the back and then closes the door between the front and the back of the plane.

"Enzo's father," Julian says.

I frown. "Enzo's father can't be financing you, he's dead."

"No, he's not financing me. He's the reason for all of this, though. He originally made a deal with Siren's parents and mine. They had all agreed to work together, sharing resources and working together in drug and weapons trade. Eventually, Enzo's father, Mr. Black, cut our families out and ensured we were powerless."

"So, this all started because your parents and Siren's parents wanted revenge against the Black family?"

"Yes, our families wanted to ruin the Black family. The box contains the ultimate tool to do that—a cancer that spreads like a virus with us having the only cure. We could control who lived and who died."

I nod, it makes sense. "But then Siren killed them all."

"Did she?" Julian sips his drink.

I frown. "She did. She told me herself."

"She tried to. And she almost succeeded, but one man survived."

"Who?"

Julian grins. "Her father."

"Siren's father is financing you?"

"Yes. He invested some money in oil. He made a killing. He wanted me to hire her so I could keep an eye on her. We never realized that she was the key to finding the box all along, though."

"If her father survived, wouldn't he have known the truth?"

"No, he thought Siren had failed in stealing the box from the Black vault. We thought you knew where the box was. We were wrong; she succeeded. We were too stupid to realize that a woman like Siren doesn't fail."

I smirk. "No, she doesn't."

"That's what I remembered. That Siren doesn't fail. I also know that you know Siren better than anyone. We may not know the exact location where she hid the box in Scotland, but you know her. If you want to find Langston before he hurts her again, we will have to work together to find her."

"Where is Siren's father?"

"Why would I tell you that? It's one of the few things keeping me alive."

"Where is he?" I threaten again.

"I'll tell you as soon as I have the box and am safely away. He's at the top of your death list, and since I want him dead too, I have no problem letting you do the dirty work."

"You're scum."

"I know. But soon, I will hold the power of the world. You could have had it, but instead, you will trade it all away for love. Who's the fool?"

I don't answer, but I know what he thinks—I'm the fool. A fool that would do anything for love.

30

SIREN

I TAKE a deep breath and gasp as I struggle to walk up the hill toward the castle at the top. Where I last saw my brother. Where I hid the box with him.

"Are you okay? Do you need me to carry you?" Langston asks.

I stop and grip my waist. "No, I'm fine. It's just this damn body armor underneath my shirt. It's not built for pregnant women. It's very tight around my chest."

Langston laughs. "You don't look pregnant anymore with how tight that thing goes around you. I can imagine it's hard to breathe in."

"Yes, but it keeps me and the little one safe, so I'll deal with it."

I take another step, and a large boom explodes right next to me. Langston jumps on top of me as he draws his gun and looks around, but there doesn't seem to be anyone nearby.

I look over to the right where the bomb went off. Close, but more of a warning than an actual attempt on our lives.

"That would be my brother," I say.

Langston frowns. "Are you sure you don't have his phone number? We could just call him and tell him we intend to destroy the box and avoid all of this."

"I wish it were that simple, but Easton promised to protect it with his life, even from me. He hoped that someday someone would come along with a pure heart, someone who could break the cure from the cancer and use it only for good."

"But that person never came along."

"No. We could drop a bomb; blow the whole castle up and then search in the wreckage to ensure it was destroyed," I say, my voice sounding cruel and harsh.

"Could you really do that with your brother inside?" Langston asks.

Maybe—that's how far I'm willing to go to protect my family and the world. But I don't say that. It's an option if it comes to that, but first, we will try to get it by convincing my brother to destroy it.

"Stay behind me," Langston says as we continue up the hill. Zeke said the same thing to me back in Spain, and we ended up separated. I hope that doesn't happen again.

More bombs rain down around us, but none of them come close enough to cause us any danger, so we continue on up the hill. I hope that as much as I don't want to kill my brother, he doesn't want to kill me either.

We make it to the top of the hill in one piece, standing in front of the looming castle. It looks like we've gone back in time. Other than a few vines growing higher on the side of the castle, it's just as it was when I was last here.

"Ready?" Langston asks me.

I nod.

"You know that you don't have to come. I can meet with your brother on my own," he says.

"I know, but if he's going to listen to anyone, it will be me."

We both walk with our guns up to the castle. Langston won't let me get too close to the door, as he knocks, in case it's booby-trapped.

There is no answer, so Langston picks the lock and opens the door. He points his gun in as he enters the house, motioning for me to wait.

A moment later, he returns to the door and waves me inside. I step in and a cold chill courses through me. If anyone is living here, they live a very cold, empty life.

"Easton, it's Aria, your sister. We just want to talk," I say, hoping that if my brother is somewhere in the house, he'd respond to me.

We creep around the large, seemingly abandoned castle, until a voice stops us in our tracks.

"You should leave."

We turn around, trying to find where the voice is coming from, but I can't tell.

"Do you see where he is?" I whisper to Langston.

"No," he replies, his eyes peering around, trying to find him.

"We want to destroy the box. I should have never left it here. I should have destroyed it," I say.

Suddenly, a man steps forward from the shadows—my brother.

"Easton?" I say.

"Yes," he responds.

I lower my gun, then push Langston's down, although Langston doesn't seem happy with it. He keeps his gun aimed at Easton's feet.

"You don't have to give us the box. Just destroy it in front of us. Or go destroy it and bring back the box if you wish.

But there are evil men coming for it. They could be hours or minutes away. We have to destroy it—now," I say.

"I can't," Easton says.

I frown. "Why not? I know I thought it was best to keep it around in case someone figured out a way to use the cure without unleashing the virus, but that opportunity has passed. We have to destroy it."

Easton steps forward, ignoring Langston until he's right in front of me. "It's good to see you again, little sis. I wish I could help you, I really do, but I swore to you a long time ago that I wouldn't. I said I would protect the box, and that's what I'm doing. Only someone who truly wants the box can get it. Only someone who is willing to give up everything, sacrifice the love of their life, and their own life will be able to send the box to someone."

"What did you do with the box?"

Easton doesn't speak, but his eyes tell me. They shoot across the ocean to an island through the window. He hid it there, not here.

"Don't go after it. It's perfectly safe, Aria. There is no reason to go," Easton says.

I bite my lip and close my eyes. It's not his fault. He did what I asked and protected it with everything he has. "The box may be safe, but the men coming for it won't stop coming after my family until they have the box or it's destroyed. The only way you can help save me from these terrible men and the world from the virus is to tell me how to get the box."

Easton looks at me and then Langston.

I turn to Langston. "Leave us alone, please."

"Siren, I can't. I—"

"It's okay, Easton won't hurt me. We just need to talk, sibling to sibling."

"I'll be right outside the door," Langston says, giving Easton a stern look and then walking outside.

"Tell me, Easton. Please, we are on the same side. Tell me what I need to do to destroy the box."

Easton steps forward and whispers in my ear, afraid Langston will hear. I listen carefully, my heart thudding wildly with fear and pain at what must happen, and who must do it.

Once Easton finishes talking, he walks to the front door to let Langston back in. When he opens the door, a bullet flies at his chest.

Easton falls down dead in front of me.

"No!" I scream at the sight.

I turn to look at the door, afraid to see what I'll see when I look. But I look anyway.

"Daddy?"

31

ZEKE

JULIAN and I stare up at the hill with Julian's men surrounding us.

"Siren's here, good work. We will ensure she stays safe as long as you help me get the box," Julian says.

I don't say anything. He's crazy if he thinks I'm handing him over the keys to the virus that could kill millions of people—not going to happen.

But I need Siren alive. And for the moment, I'll do anything to keep her alive, so I keep my mouth shut.

I tracked the plane Siren and Langston got on, then had Enzo and Kai track the car they rented here. Enzo and Kai tracked them here.

We start up the hill as bombs start going off all around us. It's a minefield heading up the hill. If I'm lucky, one of them will kill Julian, and I'll have one less person to worry about. But if he's dead, Siren's father could just hire another man to come after us. As good as I am with security and tracking people down, I know it can take a lifetime to find someone who doesn't want to be found. That's not the life I want for Siren and me, so I'll let Julian live until he's no longer useful, then I'll kill him.

Julian and I make it up the hill. By my estimate, less than half the men we started with join us. We both gasp for air, but we don't get a chance to catch our breath. I spot Langston standing outside the giant castle at the top of the hill.

We both raise our guns in his direction.

"Where is Siren?" I shout at him.

Langston looks at me, then Julian. He realizes neither of us is on his side, not anymore. He betrayed us both, and now he'll pay for what he did.

"Where the fuck is she?" Julian yells, growing impatient.

Julian won't be the one who kills Langston. What Langston did is personal. If anyone kills him, it will be me.

I fire my gun in Langston's direction, purposefully missing just enough to scare him into answering my question. Instead of answering or fighting me, Langston starts running.

Without thinking, I chase after. I fire another warning shot at him as he runs around the back of the castle. Hopefully, he's leading me to Siren. A moment later, a firefight breaks out behind me.

I glance behind me in time to see Enzo and Kai leading a cavalry of men and women toward the house. Julian's small army won't stand a chance. But then droves of men are suddenly coming to join Julian's men—Siren's father's army, no doubt.

Fuck.

Langston keeps running, and I continue chasing him around the back of the castle, needing to know where he hid Siren. I want answers. I want to torture him for what he did, although there isn't time for that.

We make it to the other side of the castle, away from the fight.

"Where is Siren?" I yell at him.

Langston ignores me and turns his back to me, as he stands on the edge of the hill, looking me straight in the eyes. I aim my gun at his heart.

"Where is she?"

He jumps.

I run over to the edge where he jumped and see him sliding down the side of the hill, the slick wet grass making it easy to slide down.

I get a running start then start sliding down the hill, hoping my added speed and weight help me to catch up to him.

We reach the bottom of the hill almost at the same time, but Langston has a slight head start on me. He's faster than me, and I'll never catch him on foot.

Where is he going?

He runs faster down to the beach.

"Why did you do it?" I yell.

He keeps running, while my heartbreak continues to drive me. I suspect it is a feeling that I will have to live with for the rest of my life. Here on out will be either great heartache or times of anger; I don't think I will ever be at peace. I will never experience anything between heartache and explosive anger again.

I fire again, and this time I hit Langston in the back. He falls, and now I have a chance to run up to him.

He rolls onto his back, breathing hard. He doesn't try to get up, even though I can see from where his shirt rode up that he's wearing protective gear under his clothes. The shot just knocked the wind out of him; it didn't penetrate his skin. So I don't know why he stopped running.

"Why?" I say again, through my anger.

Langston looks at me. "I can't. Not yet."

"You can't what?"

Langston shakes my head. "Shoot me if you have to. Do it, but it won't save Siren."

"Where is she?"

"The question you should be asking is how to save her."

I frown. "What the hell is that supposed to mean?"

"The box isn't here."

"Where?"

Langston glances behind him, and I spot the island out in the distance. The box is there. *Why is Langston telling me this?*

I hold the gun to Langston's head. He either tells me the truth now, or I'll kill him, just like he killed my child.

"Zeke!" Siren's voice rings behind me. I turn just in time to see her with fear in her eyes. When I turn back, Langston is gone.

But Siren is alive. I can see her. That's all that matters.

32

SIREN

"DADDY?" I stare at the man standing in the doorway of the castle. My brother lies on the floor.

"Yes, it's me."

Jesus.

I lean down and put my finger to Easton's pulse. I feel nothing. He's dead from a single shot.

A tear forms in my eye for the brother I never got to know. A brother who became a hermit so my parents wouldn't use him for their own means—a brother who committed his life to protecting me and the box.

Gone, just like that.

I stand back up and look at my father. There are more wrinkles around his eyes since the last time I saw him, and his head is almost completely covered by gray hair.

"You didn't have to kill him, you know," I say, my anger on full display.

He ignores me and steps into the castle over Easton's body.

I could run, but I don't. I need to understand my father's

role in this, and how he's alive when I thought I killed him along with my mother.

"Is Mom—?" I ask.

"Dead. You managed to get that part right."

"How are you alive?"

"The same way your boy toy is alive. You threw me in the water with a bullet in the chest and expected me to die. But an angel came along and saved me."

"You've been behind everything. You're financing Julian's ventures."

"I am, not that the money has been very well spent so far."

"Why?"

"My mission never stopped. I've always wanted the virus. I've wanted to control its cure, to decide who is worthy of living and who isn't. It's the only way to ensure the world survives. There are too many dangerous, evil people in this world."

"Yes," I hiss. "People like you."

"Oh, my dear Aria. Or should I call you Siren? That's what you call yourself now, right? A siren. Doesn't sound like you've turned to the good side, my dear."

I ignore him, which only pisses him off.

"Where is the box?"

"Maybe you shouldn't have killed Easton, and he would have told you."

He grabs my arm. "Where is it, Aria?"

He moves to strike me, but I stop him, shoving his arm back. "I'm not a child anymore, Father. I know how to protect myself. I know how to fight back."

"And I have an army of men just outside that will kill you if you so much as step foot outside the castle. You're stuck with me inside. Where is the box?"

I shove him back. "I'm not afraid of your army."

He lands a punch before grabbing my neck and shoving me hard into the stone wall behind me. "You should be. You should be very afraid, my dear daughter."

"You're a monster. You killed your own son. And now you want to kill your daughter."

"If I have to, yes. I don't enjoy killing like your lot do, but I will do whatever it takes in order to reach my goal."

"Well, we have that in common then, Father."

I head-butt him, and he releases me. I have my gun in the back of my pants. I could shoot and kill him dead and be done with this mess, but I don't. This is personal between us. I want him to know how strong I am before he dies. I want him to know what he missed by going after this ridiculous mission instead of being a good father to me.

My father steps back, surprise in his eyes. He pulls out his phone, I'm sure to call for help.

"Really? I'm just a girl. Don't think you can fight me one on one?"

He frowns and puts his phone away. "I just didn't want you to get hurt." He rolls up his sleeves, and I roll my eyes. He seriously thinks he's going to win this fight. He doesn't know me at all; he never did.

He swings at me, and I dodge it easily. His swings are slow and lazy. The mark of a man who never has to fight. His men do that for him.

He swings again, and this time I let his fist brush the side of my ear.

He smirks like he's won. I haven't fought back yet. I'm buying my time, letting him think he's powerful before I make my move.

But I won't let him hurt me.

When he reaches into his pocket, pulls out a flask to drink, and then throws whiskey into my eyes, I lose it.

I can't see, my eyes burn from the liquor, but that won't be a problem to take down my father.

I punch him in the gut, knocking the wind out of him. Then I kick his legs, knocking them out from beneath him. I twist his arm behind his back as I drag him to the staircase in the center of the foyer.

I blink rapidly, trying to get the alcohol out of my eyes, and then wipe it on my sleeve.

"You bitch," my father growls.

"No, I'm not a bitch."

I leave him for a second as I grab one of the frayed curtains and then use it to restrain his arms behind his back and tie him to the staircase.

"You're no father of mine. You never were." I spit on him. "I hope you burn in hell."

I start to walk away when he says, "Still not strong enough to finish the job, I see. You just leave me here tied up. I could escape death once again."

I turn with an evil grin. "You could, but I'm much stronger than I was before. And trust me, before the day is over, you'll be burning down with this castle."

I walk away, headed toward the front door, stopping at Easton's body.

"I'm so sorry, brother. Rest in peace."

And then I walk out the door.

There is a battle ensuing, but I don't see anyone I recognize. I need to get to the box. Easton told me where it is—on the small island across the channel.

I sneak around the edge of the castle with my gun drawn. I spot the island through the fog and head in that direction, when two men at the edge of the water draw my attention.

Langston is on the ground, and Zeke stands above him with a gun to Langston's head. Zeke doesn't understand the truth. He doesn't know what Langston has done, so I can't let Zeke shoot him.

"Zeke!" I yell, giving Langston a moment to get away. But when Zeke looks at me, all I see is Zeke, and my heart leaps to him, trying to comfort the pain I know he's in.

I start running toward him.

33

ZEKE

SIREN STARTS RUNNING down the hillside while I run up the beach. I catch her as she jumps from the bottom of the hill into my open arms.

"I was so scared that Langston hurt you," I say, holding her close.

"Just as I was worried that Julian hurt you."

I hug her tighter. I wish we could stay like this forever, but there is a battle happening just up the hill. Langston is gone. Julian is loose and possibly has already found the box. And her father is who knows where.

"We have to get to the island," Siren says.

I nod, already knowing this from Langston. "Let's go."

I grab her hand and pull her down the beach to the small wooden boat stuck in the sand. "Get in."

"Won't you need help to get it in the water?"

"No, get in."

Siren jumps into the small sailboat just as a crack of lighting bursts overhead. A storm has moved in right over us, and its dark, heavy rain clouds are about to drown us with rain. Of course, the world couldn't make this easy for us.

I push with all my might, my feet digging into the sand as I push the sailboat into the water. Siren, of course, already has the sail up as I hop into the boat.

I come up behind her, helping her to guide the sail and giving me an excuse to hold her.

"I love you so much, Siren. So much." I kiss her neck.

"I love you, too. But we aren't going to say goodbye again. We are going to battle this together. Even if we are separated, it's not the end; it's not goodbye."

I turn her head and kiss her on the lips. "I agree, no more goodbyes."

I kiss her again, knowing that even though we won't say goodbye, this could still be our last kiss, so I make it worth it.

As we kiss, the rain falls around us. The winds pick up and thunder rolls through.

Together we grab the sail and hold on, trying to get the wind to push us toward the island. But the wind is hitting us from the side, pushing us further out to sea instead of toward the island. It's going to be a battle in this weather to get us to the island, or even near enough to jump and swim.

I have to let Siren go so we can both go yank on the sails. The rain pours down in sheets, until we are both soaked.

"Steady the boom," Siren shouts through the wind.

"Get in front of the tiller," Zeke says.

The boat rocks hard and back forth. This tiny boat wasn't meant to withstand this level of storm. We shouldn't have taken this boat out, but it's too late for that now.

That's when I see the other boat coming—yacht, to be exact.

"Siren," I shout through the rain. She looks at me, and I point in the distance. She sees the yacht as well.

We don't know who is driving the yacht—Julian, Enzo, or Kai.

We don't know if help or danger is coming toward us.

"We have to get to the island," Siren says, not wanting to wait to find out the intentions of the yacht.

I know what she's about to suggest, and I hate it.

"No," I say.

She lets go of the rope she's holding. The boat rocks hard as she walks to me. "Get me to the island. I'll get the box. It's the safer job," she says.

I rub my arms up and down her arms, knowing none of this is safe.

"Kill Julian," she continues.

"I can't until—"

"My father is tied up in the castle. Tell Enzo or Kai to blow it up."

I blow out a breath. I can barely see her through the rain. It's impossible to see or feel anything but the heavy rain.

"Just get me close to the island," she says.

"I'm not dumping you in the ocean in the middle of a storm."

"Yes, you are. I'm a big girl. I can swim."

She kisses me again.

"And don't kill Langston, promise me. Not until I return with the box."

"Why? I have to kill him after what he did to you and..." I can't bring myself to finish without turning into a blubbering mess.

"I know, and he'll pay for what he did. But I need to be there when it happens. Promise me," she says.

"I promise," I say, although I don't understand it.

"Kill Julian; I'll destroy the box," Siren says.

"And then we will live happily ever after in our forever."

She kisses me hard, yanking on the rope to turn us hard toward the island.

It takes all my strength to let her go, but I have to. If Julian is on that yacht, I don't trust that she will be safe.

I watch her dive into the ocean; she's close enough to the island now to make it. I watch nonetheless as she swims through the waves. Siren is an excellent swimmer, and for once, the waves seem to be working in our favor, pushing her quickly toward the island.

I wait until I see her standing on the beach, and then I turn toward the yacht that is still headed toward me, and I make a stand. Julian will not get to the island. He will have to go through me first. And finally, I have the power to kill him.

34

SIREN

I STAND on the island as I look back at Zeke. I'm terrified that we are going to lose, and that I just lost my chance to explain to Zeke what truly happened. But now wasn't the time to explain to him the truth, the sin I committed.

He has a battle to fight against Julian, and I have a battle to fight inside this castle against the obstacles that Easton setup. He told me the main keys to getting through the castle and obtaining the box, but it doesn't guarantee that I'll survive, especially given the final obstacle.

I stare up at the ruined castle. While the castle on the mainland was complete, this one is in pieces, although twice the size.

I grip my stomach, knowing the cost of failing. Zeke would never forgive me. I would never forgive me.

I won't fail. I can't.

Just like Zeke won't.

Or Enzo and Kai.

I walk carefully to the edge of the castle. There are three main security obstacles in place before getting to the final room, where the box and one final obstacle wait. The three main obstacles don't seem too hard. The hard part is figuring out which room the box is hidden in and then claiming it.

The first room is the easiest—lasers.

I open the door to the old castle. It feels the opposite of modern. It shouldn't have a security system like this in it. I don't know how Easton managed to build such a feat, but I'm guessing it took him years to build this.

I take one step, and the lasers turn on. I take a deep breath as the lasers come near but never touch me.

I've got this.

Two steps forward.

Three to the left.

One forward.

Two to the right.

I repeat the steps Easton gave me, with the memory of him saying he would never help me playing in the back of my head. I hope his instructions are the truth and not a trap.

I take my final step out of the room and exhale a breath. *First obstacle down.*

The next is deciding which of the three doorways to head through.

When in doubt, follow your heart, Easton's voice rings through.

I step forward into the center room. That's what my heart tells me, so that's where I go.

This is one of the rooms I'm dreading. The smoke that starts billowing confirms that I chose the correct room. The door behind me slams shut, locking me in here.

You have sixty seconds once the door closes to pick the lock at the other end before the smoke kills you, Easton's voice reminds me.

I run to the other end of the room, coughing as the smoke begins to enter my lungs. I pull out a hairpin and go to work on the door. There are three separate locks—two deadbolts and one on the doorknob.

I start on the two deadbolts first.

The first unlocks.

Then the second.

I have plenty of time left to unlock the third and easiest one, but the pin breaks off in the lock.

"Fuck," I cough.

I try to use my nails to dig it out, but it's stuck. I rattle the door handle, but it doesn't budge.

I feel my lungs fill up with toxic smoke. It burns worse than the last time I breathed in smoke like this. This smoke is ten times as toxic.

My body wants to crumble to the ground.

You promised me, don't give up, Zeke's voice echoes in my head.

I keep myself standing, and I study the door as best as I can through the smoke. I can't find any weaknesses in the door. The door isn't too thick. *Maybe I can break it down?*

I kick the door as hard as I can. It only makes a small dent, but it gives me enough motivation to keep trying. I kick over and over, hoping it's enough to make a crack that will give me a means to escape.

I cough harder, my head growing dizzy and light. It won't be long until I pass out, and I won't be able to make it out of here alive.

Suddenly, the door is thrown open, and a man's hands grab me and pull me out of the room.

We both cough loudly several times as we grip the floor.

"Can we agree that you won't walk into a room filled with smoke anymore?" Langston says between coughs.

"Thanks for saving me again."

"You don't need to thank me for saving you."

I smile at him until I see the blood and sweat covering him. "Langston! You're hurt. What happened?"

He rests on his back as he slumps against the hallway. I lean against the wall next to him.

"The next room got the better of me."

I frown and remember what Easton said. *Bullets capable of penetrating any armor.*

He nods.

I pull his shirt open, until I find a bullet lodged in his chest. "Oh, God."

"It looks worse than it is. It missed my heart. But I failed, I couldn't get the box."

"If you hadn't had failed, you wouldn't have been here to rescue me."

He smiles at that.

I rip the bottom of my shirt off and use it as a bandage to wrap around his shoulder. "Do you have a way to contact Enzo and Kai and let them know where you are?"

"Yes."

"Good." I stand up, my head no longer pounding, and I'm able to stifle a cough.

"Don't go, Siren."

"I have to."

"No, you don't. You could die. The next room is no joke. I won't be able to come in and save you. You'd be on your own."

"Call Enzo and Kai. Tell them to be ready to pick you up soon."

"Pick *us* up," Langston says.

I turn and walk to the next room.

"Siren! Don't!" Langston tries to get off the floor, but he's too weak from blood loss.

I can't think about Langston. All I can think about is Zeke and our future. I have to do this, so that we will have a future instead of living in constant fear. I have to protect Zeke.

35

ZEKE

THE YACHT CONTINUES STRAIGHT at me. And if I didn't know before, I know now who is driving the yacht—Julian.

If it were Enzo or Kai, they would have turned by now instead of ramming the side of my tiny sailboat.

I brace for impact. I could jump into the water, but I'm tired of being in the ocean. I'd rather stay standing for as long as possible, even if I'm just as soaked on this boat as I would be in the water.

I hold on tightly as the yacht hits my small boat—the sound of the wood breaking cracks as loud as the lightning. The yacht drives through the heart of my boat. And just before it pierces me, I jump, grabbing onto one of the ropes hanging from the side of the yacht. I quickly begin climbing up the side of the yacht as more thunder cracks over and over, the weather warning me of the danger ahead.

I reach the top of the yacht and am immediately punched in the head. I take the hit but stumble backward.

"I thought we were on the same side," I say.

Julian laughs. "We were never on the same side. We were always just using each other to get what we wanted."

I pull out my gun and start shooting at him. He ducks, avoiding the spray.

"Where is the box?" Julian pulls out a grenade launcher and aims it my way.

"Go to hell," he says.

I dive just as he shoots it, blowing a large hole into the ship.

"Really? Going to hide behind a gun instead of fighting me face to face?"

"I really don't care how I kill you, just that I do." He fires again, blowing another huge hole.

Kill him, Siren's words play through my head on repeat. *Blow up the castle.*

Julian's gun is out of rounds, and he fumbles with finding ammunition. I pull out my phone and type a quick message to Kai and Enzo to blow up the castle and then pick Siren up on the small island.

Julian has changed to using a machine gun to fire at me as I hide behind a wall. *Thank goodness the entire ship is bulletproof.*

I look up at the sky, trying to come up with a way to kill this psycho.

The storm picks up the wind, until I have to grip the door handle behind me to keep from blowing overboard. The ship moves far out, away from the land.

I hear an explosion and see smoke in the distance.

Enzo and Kai succeeded in their first mission. Hopefully, Siren did too. Now it's just up to me.

I don't hear any more bullets. Julian must have moved inside where it's safer.

I yank open the door and throw myself inside, out of the wind and rain—the boat rocks in the huge swells. I know how strong these boats are, and I know how much force it will take to bring one down. But the sounds the boat is making, the creaking, and the screeching have me worried.

A bullet whizzes past me. I've found Julian.

I run after him, shooting whenever I spot him. I catch his shoulder. He fires back as the yacht lurches sideways. I take an incorrect step, and the bullet hits my chest, knocking the wind out of me.

Don't stop. Kill him. And then come back to me.

I march forward, chasing Julian through the ship, us both exchanging shots at each other.

We reach the bridge just in time to see lightning strike the yacht igniting a fire. We both realize the yacht is sinking.

Julian tries to fire his gun at me, but he's out of bullets.

I fire my last shot back, hitting him in the leg. There is nowhere for him to run. I toss my gun down, and then I run at him with all the rage he's caused me, for all the pain and heartbreak. I put everything into it. I do it for Enzo, for Kai, for Siren, for myself, and for the baby we lost.

I should think of a way to save myself. The yacht is going down, sinking to the depths of the sea. I have no way to know where we are or how far we've been swept out to sea, but I know that we have been pushed far out with the storm.

Instead, I'm focused on my mission—killing Julian.

My body collides with his. I run into him so hard that we break through a glass window and fall hard into the ocean, my body slamming down hard on top of his. The water engulfs us; the waves crash down one on top of the other. If I don't kill Julian, the storm will, and I'll end up dead in the process.

We both kick for the surface, while fighting to push the other down, as we are desperate for oxygen.

We both crack the surface at the same time. The water

continues to hit us over and over, and it becomes more of a battle of survival than a battle with each other.

This has to change. The only way I have a chance at surviving is to kill Julian. Then I can find a way to save myself.

So when the waves hit us next, I grab onto Julian and hope that my large body can hold more oxygen than his. I pull him down into the ocean with me and hold onto his legs, hoping he didn't get a good breath.

He kicks against me, but I hold my grip tighter, knowing that I'd rather him die along with me than let him get another ounce of air.

He kicks hard, but I pull him deeper into the ocean as my lungs start to tell me they need oxygen. Fear and anxiety start racing through me, but I let it fuel me to sink further down instead of going up.

Julian is getting desperate above me. Desperate for oxygen, for last words before he dies, but he'll get neither.

He digs into his pocket, and I see the shininess of the knife that he holds. But if I let go, he'll get away. He stabs my hand. I grip my teeth tighter together to ensure I don't let any spare oxygen out. He drives the knife again and again into my hand, but I hold on. We are close. He's using too much energy. He will run out of oxygen soon.

Julian looks at me with desperation and a wildness in his eyes. If he's going to die, he wants me to die with him.

I know what's coming, and I brace myself.

His knife slices through my neck, a wound that unleashes plenty of blood. I need oxygen. Now, if I'm going to survive.

Instead, I hold on, praying that my oxygen supply doesn't run out. When I can't hold on any longer, I let go and kick to the surface. I hit the air, still filled with pouring down rain, expecting Julian to hit the surface a second later. But he doesn't.

I look down into the water and watch as his body drifts down—Julian's dead.

I take a deep, calming breath—*Julian Reed is dead.*

Finally, I succeeded.

I hold my hand to my neck, hoping to stop the blood as I look around, trying to find out where I am. The storm is still beating down on me, and I can't see very far, but I don't see land. I don't see any boats. It's just me, once again in the middle of the ocean all alone while I bleed to death.

The truth broke us.

Love destroyed us.

Sin saved us.

How far will I go for love?

As far as it takes...and in my case, saving Siren means I'm to once again die in the ocean. But I have no regrets.

I died for the love of my life.

36

SIREN

TRUST YOUR HEART, Easton's voice rings in my head.

I step into the room and look at all the guns lining the walls. Guns capable of penetrating the armor I'm wearing. I could end up shot just like Langston.

Trust your heart.

My eyes say to stick to the right and move as quickly through the room as possible. But my heart says to take it slow, one step at a time, and to stay by the walls.

I move to one side of the wall and take a careful step. The guns start, but I'm able to jump and avoid getting hit. The guns reload before firing higher this time, and I duck.

I take a deep breath. *I can do this.*

Step by step, I do the same. One step forward and dodge the bullet spray before moving on to the next. Everything in my body is telling me to run, but then I can't watch the guns change direction a second before firing. I won't know to duck or jump to avoid being shot.

Finally, I take my last step out of the room. I've survived in one piece.

Now I just have to find which of the many ruined rooms left that the box is in, and survive the final test.

"Okay, Easton, where did you hide it?"

There are five rooms left. Two are open to the sky, and the rain continues to pour down. The other three have roofs.

The smart thing would be to hide the box in one of the more complete rooms, but something hidden shouldn't be obvious.

I step into the room on the far left. It's the most incomplete, the least obvious room. I shield my eyes from the rain as I look around for where he hid it. *Surely, he didn't just bury it in the ground.*

My hands go against the walls, and I find a crevice that my hand fits in perfectly. I slip my hand in and all of a sudden, the room is moving. New walls are going up, the floor shifts, and a roof starts covering overhead. And just like that, I'm in a high tech room.

Easton went all out to protect the box, as he should have.

I just don't know if I'm worthy of getting the box. I asked him to protect it, even from me, so the last test will test me as well as anyone else.

A computer comes up from the ground with the highest tech safe I've ever seen. I don't see a door on it or any mechanism that could be cracked.

I walk over to it and try to lift it, but I can't move the safe as I expected. The only way to get the box is to complete the last test. I look around the room—no doors, no windows, no escape. I won't be getting out of here until I complete the test either.

I look at the computer screen on the safe, my new enemy.

I know what is about to happen—Easton told me. But I still haven't figured out how to solve his puzzle. All he told me was that wanting to destroy the box wasn't enough to open it.

Suddenly, the screen comes alive, and the computer voice speaks. "Are you here for the box?"

I walk to the screen and press the button that says, "Yes."

"How far are you willing to go?"

I stare at the screen, my mind whirling. Easton told me that I would have to give up everything if I wanted to get the box.

I rest my hand against my stomach, feeling my baby kick. I think about Zeke on the yacht, who has hopefully killed Julian by now.

I don't want to lose either of them. I'm not willing to lose either of them.

I will do what it takes to protect them, yes. But I won't give them up to get this box. I won't give them up to save the world.

A symbol pops up on the screen, telling me that it's listening to my voice. Now is the time to speak. I see the guns come out; all pointed at me. I see the timer on the wall with a countdown.

If I answer incorrectly, the guns will go off, the room will be destroyed, and the box will be gone forever. It's what I want, the box gone. But I don't want to sacrifice my child to save the world.

My child is more important.

My love is more important.

Follow your heart.

"I'm not willing to go far at all for a stupid box. I'm not willing to give up my family, my husband, my child, my love. I won't give up the love of my life to protect the world. All I'm willing to do is give up myself, lose my own life to get the box. But I can't even do that since my life is tied to another. How far will I go for a stupid box? Not far at all. How far will I go for those I love? As far as it takes."

I close my eyes, not having a clue if I said the right words or not. I wait for the bullets. I wait for the guns, the bombs. I wait for death.

But it doesn't come.

I open my eyes, thinking maybe I've already died, when I see the screen swirling. The safe unlocks, the room opens. I did it. I'm free.

I grab the box from the safe and then run out of the room before the guns accidentally go off.

As I step foot outside of the castle, I hear the whirl of a helicopter. I look up and find Enzo, Kai, and Langston peering down at me. *Thank God.*

I wave at them, and the helicopter lands next to me. I climb in.

"Where's Zeke?" I ask Langston, sitting in the back next to me and his arm bandaged up properly now.

"We are going to search for him now. The yacht got pushed out to sea in the storm. We'll find him," Langston says.

Kai and Enzo give me a look, and then we are flying over the ocean. I hand Langston the box to keep safe, while I look out the window in search of Zeke.

Three hours later and we still haven't found him.

All eyes are on me.

"We aren't giving up," I say, firmly.

"We aren't asking you to," Kai says gently.

"Then what are you asking?"

"I'm telling you that we are almost out of fuel. We are going to have to head toward land to refuel and make a better plan to find him."

My tears come back, but I choke them back. I have to be strong for Zeke. I have to.

"We won't give up. We've given up on Zeke before, we won't again," Enzo says.

I look around at the three people outside of me who care about Zeke the most. We will find him. We have to.

37

ZEKE

It's been three days.

Somehow I'm still alive, still floating in the water.

I'm delusional. I won't last much longer. My body is too weak. If it was up to my heart, I'd fight forever, but my heart isn't in control anymore. My lungs are, and they are about to give out.

And then I hear a new sound out of nowhere. All I've heard for days are waves, wind, and the occasional bird. But this, this is heavenly.

It's not real, I know it. I'm dying; the beautiful sound is my brain easing my pain as I take my last breaths. I'm thankful.

I hear a splash and look over, assuming I'll find a dolphin or, with my luck, a shark.

Something is swimming toward me—my angel.

"Zeke!" I hear her scream as she grabs onto me. "Oh my god!"

Her hand goes to my neck immediately, but the wound stopped bleeding long ago.

"You're alive," she cries.

"My angel, my beautiful angel."

She laughs through her tears. "No, your Siren. I've been calling out to you for days. I finally found you, time to go home."

"This is the best dream ever," I say.

She shakes her head and then pulls me hard. Next thing I know, I'm being lifted onto something hard that rocks. It doesn't make sense to me, but it doesn't matter, I won't be conscious much longer.

"We need to get him to a hospital, now," a voice says.

"Hold on, baby. Just hold on. Keep your promise to love me forever," Siren says, and then she presses the sweetest kiss to my lips before the world goes dark.

———

I OPEN MY EYES, and all I see is light. *Am I dead? Is this heaven?*

"Zeke," I hear a voice so tentative and scared.

I turn my head, and Siren jumps on me before kissing me all over.

"You're alive. You're awake. Thank God," Siren screeches as she kisses me everywhere.

"I am, it seems. Thanks to you."

She kisses me once more before curling up next to me in what I realize is a giant bedroom on a beach that looks an awful lot like Miami.

"You're home in Miami," Siren says, answering my unspoken question.

"And everyone?"

Siren whistles, and the door opens. Enzo and Kai walk in. Kai has tears flowing from her eyes, while Enzo tries and fails to hold his back.

"You're alive! We were so worried," Kai says.

"Come here, Stingray." I hold out my arm to her and pull her into a hug, while Siren lies on the bed next to me, still holding onto me.

"So glad you made it through," Enzo says, avoiding eye contact so he doesn't start crying.

"When you heal, you'll come back to work for us, won't you?" Kai asks.

"I need to discuss it with Siren first, but I know that I won't want to be stepping foot on a yacht or on the ocean anytime soon."

Everyone laughs at that.

"Come on, Stingray, we should give them some time alone," Enzo says, pulling Kai off me. Together they walk out of the room.

"Julian? Your father?" I ask Siren.

"Both dead."

"Your brother?"

"Dead."

"I'm so sorry."

"I'm sorry my brother's gone, but I know this is what he wanted, to die protecting what he knew he should and saving the world."

"You saved the world," I say, kissing her hand.

"With some help."

I smile at that.

"And Langston?" I feel the anger and pain returning at his name.

"He'll be in to visit soon."

I frown. "I'm going to kill him."

"Wait, listen first."

I narrow my eyes as she takes my hand and puts it under her shirt to her stomach.

"What are you doing?"

"Just wait."

A second later, I feel a kick.

"Oh my god! The baby?"

"Is alive."

I pull her tighter to me. "How? I thought Langston hurt you and the baby. I thought—"

"No, he realized when we got back to the room that night that Julian was watching. He needed to make my reaction as real as possible, so he did the minimum to physically hurt me to make me fear him. To put on a show for Julian."

"What are you saying?"

"I'm saying Langston saved me. He didn't actually rape me, just pretended."

"But the blood?"

"I caused it. I found a knife and used it to cut both Langston and my thigh to cause all the blood, so you'd think I'd lost the baby."

"But why?"

"I needed to see you broken to trigger my memories, and that was the most traumatic thing I could think of. I'm so sorry."

"Shh, you have nothing to be sorry for." I rub her stomach. "In fact, you just made me the happiest man to know that you're still pregnant. We are going to get our happily ever after finally."

And then I kiss her, and kiss her, and kiss her, long into the night.

Until a knock at the door draws our attention away from each other.

Langston pokes his head in. "Sorry to interrupt, but I think it's time we destroyed this since we all risked our lives to get it."

Siren stands and helps me out of the bed, although I don't really need the help. I do enjoy being so close to Siren, though.

Langston looks at me, and I look at him with a nod. All the lies and sins we've committed will take a while to heal, but I know that he cares about Siren and that he will protect her with his life. That makes him one of the best men I know.

Langston motions for us to follow, and so we do until we are all outside on the sand—Enzo, Kai, Langston, Siren, and me.

Langston puts the box in the center of our circle along with driftwood. He douses the wood gasoline, and then he hands a box of matches to Siren.

Siren strikes one of the matches. "I should have done this long ago, then maybe we wouldn't have gone through hell."

"We got rid of two more evil men who would have continued to terrorize the world without us. It was worth it," Kai says.

Siren nods. "Still, it feels silly that I kept it around because of a feeling that it needed to exist. That time never came. Now it's time to destroy it."

And then with that, Siren tosses the match onto the wood. We all stand around the fire, watching the box and contents slowly burn.

Kai and Enzo walk back to the house. Followed by Langston. And then it's just me and Siren on the beach.

"Truth or sin, what did you do to get the box?" I ask. She's told me the story of what her and Langston did to save the baby, but not what she did to get the box, what danger she put herself in.

"Truth or sin, what did you do to kill Julian?" she asks back with raised eyebrows.

We've both done incredible things for love. We burned a castle down, lied, and hurt and killed so many people. But in the end, our love prevailed, and it will continue to prevail forever.

"Sin," we both say at the same time. The truth doesn't matter now, and sinning together is much more fun.

"Fuck me, Zeke."

I grin. "Oh, I plan to, over and over and over. Just like I plan on loving you, forever."

EPILOGUE

SIREN

"CAYDEN IS SO SWEET," Kai says as we stare over my six-week-old son. Zeke got his way in the end and got to name him, the perfect name for our little warrior.

"He is sweet when he's not crying. I don't think we've slept more than an hour these last few weeks," I say, staring down at my sleeping boy in his crib.

"It gets better, trust me. Soon you'll want these days back."

I sigh, my life couldn't get any better. Kai hugs me, holding me close to her.

"You need to take your time and enjoy your son, so this isn't the time to talk about it, but I can't wait until you get back to work. It's such a boys-fest without you."

I laugh. "We definitely need to hire more women."

"I agree."

Zeke and I have been working for Kai and Enzo these last few months. I've mainly worked from the office with Kai, while the boys have done the more hands-on work. Although, Zeke has yet to step foot back on a yacht or in the ocean. I'm sure he will as soon as our son is old enough to ask him to take him out on a boat, as we do live in Miami on the beach.

I yawn.

"Go take a nap, I'll watch this little guy for you," Kai says.

"You're a good friend."

I leave the nursery, guessing I won't get more than a twenty-minute nap in before Cayden wakes up, but I'll take what I can get.

I walk to my bedroom and close the door, when Zeke grabs me from behind, holding me in his arms.

"We're alone," he says.

"It seems we are," I respond. "Although, Kai is in the nursery. And Enzo is watching football in the living room."

"They can wait."

"Oh, yea? What do you have in mind?"

"Your doctor cleared you, right?" He kisses down my neck, and I moan.

"Yes," I breathe, forgetting how wonderful it is for him to be kissing me like this. To make me come alive with one touch. I've been so busy focusing on Cayden's every need that I forgot for a moment that I have needs.

"Can I fuck you, Mrs. Kane?"

I smile. "You sure can, Mr. Kane." Our fingers intertwine, as he lifts me and carries me to our giant bed. We got married officially, just the two of us in the courthouse a month before Cayden was born. We didn't want anyone there. In our eyes, we got married in the ocean. Something positive that I can remind Zeke of soon to coax him back into the ocean.

I look like a mess in my leggings and an oversized shirt. I

haven't showered in two days, and my hair is in a messy bun on top of my head, but Zeke doesn't care. His eyes heat all the same when he removes my shirt and leggings.

"God, I've missed you, baby," he says when he has me naked beneath me.

I grab his long hair and yank him toward me. "Shut up and fuck me."

He chuckles against my lips as he kisses me. He's trying to take his time, but now that he's reminded me what this feels like, I'm desperate for him to be inside me.

I grab his shirt, yanking it off to reveal his sexy six-pack. I'm one of the luckiest girls in the world to get to have this man any night I want. He helps me remove his pants, and then he's at my entrance in record time. His fingers tease my clit.

I grab his hips, trying to pull him inside me. "Slow, baby. I don't want to hurt you."

"You can't hurt me. It's not possible." I roll my hips, pushing his tip inside me.

He gasps, and I think he might explode from this moment alone. He bites his lip, pushing his orgasm down.

"You make me crazy, Siren."

"Then fuck me already."

With that, he eases into me. It's perfect and wonderful, and the missing piece that I didn't realize I had been forgetting.

"I love you, Siren."

He thrusts into me, and I can't speak. He starts off slow and then moves faster and faster. I can't speak; all I can do is moan, cry, and scream. *Thank God for soundproof walls.*

Then we are both coming so hard that I feel like I'm going to explode.

"I love you, too," I say when I can finally catch my breath again.

We lie in the bed until I hear Cayden crying through the baby monitor, and there is a gentle knock at the door.

We both jump up and get dressed. I assume it's Kai at the door telling me Cayden is hungry, but when I throw the door open, it's Langston.

"Lang! You made it." I throw my arms around him. We haven't seen him since the birth of Cayden.

"I was tired of your phone calls telling me to get my ass over here more."

I smile at that.

"But next time you invite guests over and decide to fuck, make sure you turn the baby monitor off," Langston says.

I blush.

Zeke dies laughing.

"It's good to see you, man." Zeke pats Langston on the shoulder. "I'll grab you a beer, and we can watch the game together."

"Be right there," Langston says as Zeke leaves us alone.

"What are you running from, Lang?"

He steps into my bedroom and shuts the door. "I'm not a good man, Ren. I don't belong in this world. I'll just bring more danger into your life."

I shake my head. "Not possible, you've saved my life so many times. And everyone else's. You're a good man."

"You don't know me that well, Ren."

"I know you better than anyone. I've seen your darkness. I know you are running from pain. From Liesel? I invited her, I want to meet her, but she never answered."

"Liesel won't answer. She's out of this life for good," Langston says, walking to the window and staring out of it.

"Maybe you should go talk to her."

"She doesn't want to talk to me."

I sigh. "I just want you to be happy. And if that isn't with the woman you love, then it should be with your family. We are your family."

He shakes his head. "I can't stay, Ren. I'm sorry. I wish I could, but I can't."

"Why?"

There is another knock. I open it, and Kai is holding a crying Cayden out to me.

"I tried to hold him off as long as I could, but he's hungry," Kai says.

I take Cayden from her. "Come on, let's go watch the game together and relax. We can talk later, Lang."

He nods, and then we all walk to the living room. I sit with Zeke and start feeding Cayden. Kai and Enzo sit, their twins climbing all over them. Langston sits off in a chair by himself.

Seeing Langston by himself shows me how hard this must be for him. He has to watch Zeke and me, Kai and Enzo live our happily ever afters, while he's alone.

Langston still hasn't told me what happened between him and Liesel, but I do know that without him facing his past, he won't be able to move on and find love again.

Kai must notice the awkwardness too. "Hey, Langston."

He turns and looks at her. "Stop moping; you'll find love soon."

"I'm not looking for love. I'm a forever bachelor. I don't need a wife or family," he says.

"Yea, yea, whatever you say. Just promise me that when you do find the love of your life, that you don't drag us into your love story and make us risk our lives, okay?" Kai says with a smile trying to lighten the mood.

Everyone laughs. Everyone but Langston. He's lost in thought.

I'm going to have to have another talk with him and get him to spill the truth to me. He owes me that.

"Look, he's smiling at us," Zeke says.

I look down at our son, who has stopped feeding. He's smiling up at us. He's perfect and has Zeke's eyes and large frame. He was over ten pounds at birth. I have no doubt at all that he's Zeke's child.

"He's going to keep us on our toes, isn't he?" I ask.

"Definitely. Any child of ours is going to be trouble."

I lean my head against Zeke's chest, my son in my arms, and my family all around. I look over at Langston, and even he is smiling at me.

"I can't wait to live our happily ever after, forever with you," Zeke whispers into my ear.

"It's here, baby. It's here. This is the first part of our forever, and I can't imagine anything better."

The End

Thank you so much for reading Zeke and Siren's story! I have a bonus epilogue scene featuring Langston and Liesel that you can read here >>> https://ellamiles.com/langston-liesel-bonus

Langston and Liesel's story will be coming Fall 2020.

Make sure you are all caught up on the Truth or Lies World!

Read Enzo and Kai's story below in the Truth or Lies series!
(You also get to read Zeke's beginning)
Taken by Lies #1

Betrayed by Truths #2
Trapped by Lies #3
Stolen by Truths #4
Possessed by Lies #5
Consumed by Truths #6

FREE BOOKS

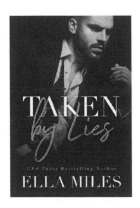

Read **Taken by Lies** for **FREE**! And sign up to get my latest releases, updates, and more goodies here→EllaMiles.com/freebooks

Follow me on **BookBub** to get notified of my new releases and recommendations here→Follow on BookBub Here

Join **Ella's Bellas FB group** to get **Pretend I'm Yours** for **FREE**→Join Ella's Bellas Here

ORDER SIGNED PAPERBACKS

I love putting my signed paperbacks on SALE!

Check them out by visiting my website:
https://ellamiles.com/signed-paperbacks

ALSO BY ELLA MILES

SINFUL TRUTHS:

TRUTH OR LIES:

DIRTY SERIES:

Dirty Revenge

Dirty: The Complete Series

ALIGNED SERIES:

Aligned: Volume 1 (Free Series Starter)

Aligned: Volume 2

Aligned: Volume 3

Aligned: Volume 4

Aligned: The Complete Series Boxset

UNFORGIVABLE SERIES:

Heart of a Thief

Heart of a Liar

Heart of a Prick

Unforgivable: The Complete Series Boxset

MAYBE, DEFINITELY SERIES:

Maybe Yes

Maybe Never

Maybe Always

Definitely Yes

Definitely No

Definitely Forever

STANDALONES:

Pretend I'm Yours

Finding Perfect

Savage Love

Too Much

Not Sorry

ABOUT THE AUTHOR

Ella Miles writes steamy romance, including everything from dark suspense romance that will leave you on the edge of your seat to contemporary romance that will leave you laughing out loud or crying. Most importantly, she wants you to feel everything her characters feel as you read.

Ella is currently living her own happily ever after near the Rocky Mountains with her high school sweetheart husband. Her heart is also taken by her goofy five year old black lab who is scared of everything, including her own shadow.

Ella is a USA Today Bestselling Author & Top 50 Bestselling Author.

Stalk Ella at:
www.ellamiles.com
ella@ellamiles.com

Made in the USA
Monee, IL
05 June 2022